ALL TUCKED INN

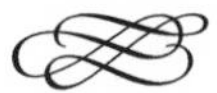

RACHEL HANNA

CHAPTER 1

The soft hum of the air conditioning and the occasional clicking of her own high heels on the marble floor were the only sounds that broke the eerie silence in the deserted office. Heather tapped her fingers against the keyboard, but the words on the screen were blurring into one another as the late night exhaustion set in.

Her Atlanta office, which was every bit the symbol of her amazing climb through the world of finance, was her sanctuary and her battleground. The walls of her office were lined with framed accolades about her work over the years, and the city skyline served as the backdrop to her often monotonous, highly successful life. Her desk was overflowing with charts, spreadsheets and file folders. Only she knew where everything was. Even her assistant had no clue.

As she got deeper into one spreadsheet, the sudden piercing sound of her phone cut through the stillness of the night, causing her to jolt upright in her chair. She looked at the caller ID and noticed that it was her mother, Lanelle. She still lived in their hometown of Jubilee, Georgia, tucked away in the Blue Ridge Mountains. Sometimes, Heather missed home. She supposed everyone did.

Still, getting an unexpected call at this hour was very rare. Her mother was not a night owl, so Heather was immediately worried.

"Hello? Mama?"

"Heather, my beautiful daughter." Lanelle's Southern drawl seemed even more prominent over the phone. "Are you working late again?"

Heather leaned against her plush leather chair, smiling slightly. No matter how far apart they were, her mother always had an uncanny ability to know when Heather was working too hard.

And, lately, she was. Maybe she was doing it to occupy her mind after a particularly bad breakup. She'd been in many relationships in her many years of life, but the last one had just about done her in. She thought they were going to get married, but instead Stephen took a job in Hong Kong and left with just a few days warning. Their entire relationship blew up right in front of her. He told her she was a workaholic, and he couldn't handle it anymore. It wasn't the first time someone had said that, but this time hurt particularly badly.

Maybe it was because she was thirty-five and never married. Maybe it was because she had watched all of her friends get married, have kids, live the whole white picket fence lifestyle. Instead, she lived in a penthouse apartment overlooking the city, and the only company she had were her half-dead plants. As much as she loved her life, it still felt lonely at times. The work she was doing just didn't fill her up like it used to.

"I have to, Mama. I've got a lot on my plate right now. We just took on two huge corporate clients, and Jim retired."

She could hear her mother's sigh all the way from Jubilee, winding through the mountain valleys and city highways before it landed in her ear on the other end of the phone. "You know, your father used to say the same thing."

The whole reason Heather had gone into finance was because of her father. Although he had passed away when she was a teenager, Heather always wanted to be like him. He was a powerful businessman, and he traveled two hours one way to his office in the city before returning to Jubilee every day. She hardly got to see him but when she did, they had such special times, fishing and hiking through the Blue Ridge Mountains. He was a different kind of man. Smart, determined, successful. But he was also a family man.

Somehow, her father had made it seem easy to be rooted in business and home at the same time. He loved the city just as much as he loved Jubilee. Of course, he hadn't been a native of Jubilee. Lanelle had, and she brought him there after they attended college together. He made it his home eventually, but he always seemed to have one foot in and one foot out.

Still, he'd loved Lanelle so much that he had moved to Jubilee just after college so Lanelle could take over the inn from her mother. All Tucked Inn had been in the family for four generations so far, and Heather definitely felt the pressure mounting for her to take it over one day.

"Honey, why don't you come home for a little bit?" Lanelle said, her voice obviously longing for her daughter to return. Heather had been gone from Jubilee for well over fifteen years now, but Lanelle never stopped trying to get her to come back. She occasionally visited, usually at Christmas, but her job kept her very busy.

"Mama, you know I can't just..."

"I'm not saying forever, dear," Lanelle interjected. "Just come for a short visit. The azaleas that you love are in full bloom in the garden and you know that the mountain air will do you good."

Heather closed her eyes for a moment and imagined the smell of the mountains this time of year. She had forgotten what the aroma of the blooming azaleas smelled like, and she had to admit that the refreshing mountain air would do her good.

"I'll think about it. I can't promise anything, but I'll try."

"That's all I ask." After chatting for a few more moments, they ended the call and Heather felt a sense of longing in her chest. She missed seeing her mother, and she wasn't getting any younger. Lanelle was seventy years old, and Heather had friends who had already lost their parents. She knew in her heart that she needed to make an effort to go home more often. After all, she was Lanelle's only child, and there was a responsibility that came with that. Her mother and father had tried for years to have a baby, and Lanelle had always referred to Heather as her little miracle child.

She stared out the office window, looking at the cityscape. She remembered when she had first moved into this office and how excited she'd been. These days, it didn't hold the charm that it used to. She closed her eyes and imagined the beautiful mountains of Jubilee, and she felt a pull she hadn't felt in a long time. Maybe it was time to go home and reconnect with everything she held dear.

She returned to her work, with her mother's words still echoing in her mind. She felt torn between two worlds, and she imagined her father had felt that for most of his adult life. That gentle whisper of home reminding her of better times was calling to her, and it might be time for her to listen. She wasn't going to stop her life in Atlanta, but she needed to go get plugged into a power source filled with family and friends. She needed the beautiful azure mountains to fill her up again. This was only temporary, she told herself, not fully believing it.

"YOU'RE DOING WHAT?" Her boss, Nathan, stared at her like she'd just announced she was joining the circus.

"I'm taking a leave of absence."

"And what if I say no?" He leaned across the desk, his elbows pressed into the dark mahogany wood, as his almost clear blue eyes glared at her. Nathan was handsome, but spooky looking.

"Then I'll take all my vacation days, which have stacked up pretty good."

"You need approval to take vacation days."

"Then I'll quit, and you'll have to deal with the Jennings file on your own." Nathan hated working with their biggest client, Steve Jennings. Heather had to admit he wasn't the easiest man to work with, and she was the only one he'd talk to. Jennings was her leverage whenever she needed Nathan to agree to something.

He gritted his teeth and groaned. "Why are you doing this to me, Heather? We're the busiest we've ever been."

"My mother needs me right now. I won't be gone long, and I can do my work remotely. Nothing will get missed. This isn't a vacation."

"Can't you hire someone to help her?"

"What?"

"When my mom got up in years, I just hired someone to go do things for her. Grocery shopping, doctor appointments, stuff like that."

"My mom doesn't need those things. Look, you're going to have to trust me on this. I need to go home."

He cocked his head to the side. "Isn't Atlanta your home?"

She paused for a moment and checked her gut. When she said home, she meant Jubilee. How was that possible after all these years?

"You know what I mean. Don't you have a hometown that you long to return to sometimes? Where times were simpler?"

Nathan let out a loud, sarcastic laugh. "Dear God, no. I grew up in the suburbs outside Boston, and I don't miss a thing about that. The big city is what I love. The traffic, the car horns, the incessant sirens going off. It's like a babbling brook to me."

Heather liked the city, but she didn't feel the same way Nathan did. In fact, all those noises annoyed the heck out of her. But she loved the convenience, the lights, and that she never felt completely alone. Except that she did feel alone, but in a much deeper way.

"I'm leaving tomorrow. I'll keep you informed on

Jennings and all my files." She stood up and walked toward the door.

"I can't believe you're doing this. You never want to leave work. You're like me, and that's why we work so well together."

He thought she was like him? Something about that made Heather very sad.

THE BUZZED BEAR was alive with laughter and talking, people clinking their glasses together and eating the hearty food. Madeline loved coming here. It was one of her favorite places in town. With its rough wooden interior and soft amber lighting, the place was a quaint hangout for the locals in Jubilee. Tonight, Madeline found herself in her favorite corner booth, sitting across from Brady, her fingers curled around a glass of wine.

Every time she looked around the room, she thought about how different her life was than just a few months ago when she first arrived in Jubilee. Originally, she was there to study small-town life so she could write a new book and get back to her big city home. Instead, she found herself knee-deep in the charm of Jubilee, falling in love with the warm people and beautiful surroundings. She looked at Brady, his eyes soft under the warm glow of the tavern lights. Every feature on his face was etched in earnestness.

"So, I've been looking at the blueprints again," Brady began, his eyes focused on the glass of beer in his hand. "The new house won't be the same as the old one. It just can't be. I want it to feel like a real home, for me, but also for Jasmine and Anna."

Madeline nodded, listening to him with her heart full of admiration. He was going through a variety of hardships, from losing his home to a fire to the sudden arrival of his estranged sister, Jasmine. She had a troubled past, and she brought with her an eight-year-old daughter, Anna, which added more layers of complexity to Brady's life.

When Madeline met him, he was a carefree bachelor running his little farm and working as a wildlife rehabilitator. Now he had no real home, and he had two new family members to take care of. From what Madeline could tell, Jasmine was still having issues, and she felt bad for Brady having to take everything on.

"They will feel at home, Brady. They say home is where the heart is, and your heart is right here in Jubilee. They will always feel at home with you."

He laughed, his eyes meeting hers. "You sound like you're writing one of your novels, Madeline."

She smiled. "It's a perk of being an author. We usually have the right words. But it is the truth. Jasmine and Anna are your family, and they will feel at home as long as you're there." She wanted to say that she felt at home as long as he was there, too, but she stopped herself. Their relationship was new, and she didn't want to make Brady think she was pushing him to go faster.

"Even if it's a small trailer that we have to live in for months while the new home is being built?"

She reached across the table, her fingers gently entwining with his. "Especially then. They're not just waiting for a house. They're rebuilding their entire lives, and you'll be able to do that together as a family."

Brady sighed. "I just hope that I'm doing all of this right. Jasmine is and has always been, a very complicated person. Anna has been through a lot. My mama would've known just how to handle all of this, God rest her soul."

"You're doing all the right things." Her thumb brushed against his. "You've given them a safe haven, and then you're going to give them a real home. You're their rock."

"No pressure, right?" he said, chuckling under his breath. She could see the weight of the world on his shoulders. Brady always wanted to do the right thing, no matter what. In situations like this, it wasn't always evident what the right thing was. She tried to say words that would comfort him, but she didn't know how he felt. She had no siblings, so she couldn't understand what it must've felt like for Brady.

His jaw twitched. "If I could get my hands on her ex-husband…"

"Don't go there, Brady. Your sister needs you, and you don't need to get thrown in jail yourself."

He nodded. "Let's just hope we never cross paths."

Silence settled between them, as they each drank their beverages and munched on chips and salsa. Laughter filled the space as a group of locals shared a joke at the bar.

"Are you ready to go?" Madeline eventually asked. She could tell that Brady was edgy, and she didn't want him to be forced to sit in a place full of laughter and conversation. She knew that when she felt worried about something, she didn't want to be in that kind of a situation. She wanted to be alone.

As they left, Madeline felt the chilly mountain air

against her skin. She wrapped her arm around Brady's, her head leaning against his shoulder as they walked down the lit streets of Jubilee. She thought of this town as her home now, and the people there were her family. Their trials and triumphs were as much hers as they were theirs.

She continued working on her small town book, weaving in real life tales. This place was no longer just the setting of her next novel but was a beautiful place to call home.

HEATHER FORGOT JUST how long the two-hour trip from Atlanta to Jubilee could seem. It would've been better if she had decided to drive in the morning, or even early afternoon. Instead, she had opted to leave after work, getting herself stuck in rush-hour traffic for a while. But then the roads opened up and led to the blue-tinged mountains before her. She had to admit, it was a sight she missed.

Even though she had grown up in Jubilee, and she was quite used to seeing mountains, they never ceased to amaze her. As a kid, she had definitely hiked many of them with her father. Occasionally, her mother would come along, but she was typically happier to stay home and spend the day baking or canning. Her mother was an incredible cook, something that Heather hadn't picked up quite as easily.

As the Blue Ridge Mountains loomed out in the distance, she could see the peaks being kissed by the setting sun, which cast a soft, golden glow that seemed to be calling her home. The sky had wisps of pink and yellow. She never got tired of seeing the beautiful sunsets that happened in those mountains. Sure, there were pretty skies in the city, but it was nothing like what she'd seen on so many nights in Jubilee.

The radio played one of her favorite songs, but her thoughts were far away. The closer she got to Jubilee, the more the memories rushed in from her childhood. Sometimes, those memories made her sad because she missed her dad. She supposed there would never be a day that she didn't. Other times, the memories made her laugh. Thoughts of old school friends, family reunions, and other activities around the inn. It truly was one of the focal points in town.

She swore she could smell the scent of her mom's famous chocolate cake, or hear the creaking of the old wooden swing that hung on the back porch of the inn. She could hear the laughter of one of her best friends from school. Sophie had moved away a long time ago, but they kept in touch on social media.

All the memories danced around in her head, causing a bit of melancholy and bittersweet feelings in the pit of her stomach. She knew that her mother was going to ask her to take over the inn, and she dreaded the conversation. How could she tell her no? How could she tell her yes?

With the skyline far away in her rearview mirror, the landscape gave way to lush forests and rolling hills. Leaving behind the hustle and bustle of the city wasn't necessarily a bad thing. Work had been particularly busy lately, and although she loved it, it was stressful. Her massage therapist said that her shoulders were becoming permanently affixed to her ears. She couldn't remember the last time she had meditated, and her yoga teacher thought she had moved away.

Heather had never been great at self-care, and it was something her mother chided her about all the time. She wanted her daughter to come home to the mountains and live a quieter lifestyle. She claimed it was better, and maybe it was. But Heather had always liked a challenge, even as a kid. She always wanted to be the best. She had always wanted her father's approval, and he had always freely given it. Still, she strived for something, and she didn't know quite what it was.

As she pulled into town, the sites greeted her like old friends. First, she saw the sign at the edge of town that said "Welcome to Jubilee." It had stood proudly for decades, but now it was a bit faded and worn. The bright blue was more of a light blue now. She saw that Perky's coffee shop was busy as usual. She couldn't wait to go there and get her favorite drinks. And then she could see the bookstore, owned by Clemmy. She loved to read. It was probably one of the few hobbies she had. She would have to make time to get by there in a few days.

The local tavern was of course alive with activity as night fell. The Rustic Spoon was full of people eating dinner, and she was sure there were all kinds of wonderful smells coming from there. These were all places that held a spot in her heart, and each one of them also held memories. The sidewalks surrounding the storefronts were the scene of many memories, including taking pictures after prom or going to one of the many festivals the town held. Each one of them made her want to smile or tear up.

As she drove up to All Tucked Inn, her heart skipped a beat. The building stood just as she had always remembered it, an elegant yet cozy structure that was at the heart of her family. Her favorite flowerbeds were in bloom, and the porch was inviting as always with its old rocking chairs and the swing that still hung at one end. It looked a bit worn, but that was to be expected for the length of time it had been hanging there. She used to sit on it every day after school with her friends, chatting about their day and all the latest school gossip.

As she stepped out of the car, she felt a bit shaky. She knew this conversation with her mother was going to be hard, because there was no way that she could come home permanently. Heather had a big career, and there was more to come. If she came back to Jubilee, her life would be at a standstill. She wouldn’t continue climbing up in her career, and she couldn't imagine living in the sleepy little mountain town for the rest of her life.

She walked up to the front door and paused for a moment, taking a deep breath. She adored her mother, but she knew that this was going to be a tough visit. This was about her family's heritage, her own connection to the past, and the choices she would make for her future.

The door suddenly opened, and there stood her mother, Lanelle Callaway. Even as she got older, she seemed to get prettier. She was tall and lean, although she had never been on a diet a day in her life. She was just one of those people who had the build of a ballerina without all the work. She had more wrinkles around her eyes and a couple of new lines between her eyes. Those always signified worry to Heather, so she figured her mother had been stressing over some things in recent years. Her hair was cut short, and it was a beautiful silver gray. Lanelle had always worn minimal makeup, but she did wear red lipstick, which was her signature.

"My baby!" she exclaimed, pulling Heather into a big hug. Heather dropped her overnight bag onto the ground with a thud.

"Mama, I've missed you." She really had. There was just something about being in the arms of her mother that made the world feel like a safer place. At the same time, Heather was well aware that her mother was getting older, and things were starting to change. Every so often she would say something that led Heather to worry she was becoming forgetful. The only saving grace was that she lived in Jubilee around people she'd known most of her life, so Heather never had to worry if her mother had help if she needed it.

"I've missed you, too. Welcome home."

One thing was for sure–Lanelle considered Jubilee to be Heather's home. No matter how many years Heather had lived in the city, Lanelle didn't accept it. She had always planned for her daughter to come back one day and take over the family business.

They stood on the porch, sunlight fading into darkness as they reconnected. As Heather looked into her mother's eyes, she saw years of hard work, love, and now a hint of desperation. The weight of the legacy of the inn had become too heavy for her mother to bear alone. Did that mean that she had to come back and carry the burden for both of them?

It wasn't that she didn't love the inn. It provided many years of wonderful memories, and she liked the idea of it. The idea of meeting new people every day. The idea of feeling her family and friends around her all the time. The idea of looking out the front door and seeing the beautiful blue-colored mountains. But she also knew what came with that. Responsibility for a business that was never going to be a big moneymaker. A smaller life without all the frills she was accustomed to.

Heather wasn't a materialistic person, but she would be lying if she said that she didn't enjoy having a nicer car, a beautiful view from her apartment, or even the ability to take trips when she wanted. Her career allowed for that, but running the inn would mean giving all of that up.

They walked inside, and Heather immediately remembered the sound of the creaking floors. There was always this one spot in the foyer, right under the picture of her great-grandfather, and she used to think when she was a kid that it was him sending a message from heaven. He had died before she was born, but her mother had kept his memory alive through stories.

She also remembered the smell. There was a mixture of peaches and pound cake, grits and collard greens. It sounded horrible, but it smelled like home. She saw the polished wood on the banister and noticed the soft glow of the lamps on the fireplace mantel in the living room. All of these brought back memories.

"Care for a cup of coffee after your long drive?" Lanelle asked as Heather followed her into the kitchen. It looked the same as it always did with its tiled countertops and brown wood cabinets. Lanelle had always been against updating it, but Heather thought it needed it. She knew it didn't need to look super modern, but an update would've done it good. Still, she had memories of this kitchen, like the gouge in the cabinet next to the microwave. Her mother had been trying to get a fly, but she did it with a spatula and caused a chip in the wood. She never did get the fly.

"Do you have decaf?" Heather asked. Lanelle turned and looked at her like she had two heads.

"Since when do you drink decaf?"

"Since last year. If I have it too late in the day, I can't sleep. And you know I already have trouble with sleeping."

Lanelle reached out and touched a strand of Heather's hair. "You shouldn't have trouble sleeping. That's because of all that stress you have in your job. Your father was the same way. Always staying up late at night with the weight of the world on his shoulders."

Heather chuckled. "And you're saying you don't stay up at night worrying about stuff?"

Lanelle sighed and turned back around to pour her a cup of coffee. "I didn't have trouble until recently." Heather decided not to pry further, but she knew her mother would eventually tell her what was keeping her up at night.

"I'll take a cup, but if I'm up at two A.M., I'm coming to get you up too," Heather said, laughing.

Lanelle poured both of them a cup and then

carried them over to the breakfast table. It looked the same as always with its weathered wood top and small vase of flowers sitting in the middle. Her mother had always loved picking flowers in the garden and putting them on the kitchen table. She said fresh flowers cured most ailments.

"I'm so glad you came."

"Me too. It's always good to come home for a visit." Heather wanted to point out that she was only there for a visit. She didn't want her mother believing that this trip meant she was staying forever. Her mother was a very persuasive woman, and Heather knew that if she didn't stand firm, she would end up giving in. "Where's Murphy?" Lanelle had adopted the dog three years ago when she saw somebody drop him out on the street. People often dumped unwanted pets in the mountains. Murphy, a mutt with a tricolor coat, benefitted from that because Lanelle had spoiled him rotten.

"One of my neighbors loves to take him for a walk after dinner. He should be home soon enough." She cleared her throat and took a sip of coffee before speaking. "I suppose you know that I want to talk to you about coming home to run the inn." Lanelle was also very abrupt and blunt. She wasn't one who was known for beating around the bush.

"Mama, can I get at least one night under my belt? I'm tired from the drive and from working. I'd like to get settled in before we have a big dust up about this."

"Of course, honey. Your room is all ready. I made your bed, and there are fresh towels in the linen closet."

"Thank you. I'm looking forward to a good night of sleep."

"Are you hungry? I have leftovers from dinner."

"No, thank you. I had a granola bar in the car."

Lanelle rolled her eyes at that. "And I don't know why you think we're going to have a big dust up, as you called it. I just want to have a chat with my daughter."

Heather smiled, raising an eyebrow as she took her first sip of coffee. "Yes, because Lanelle Callaway is known for taking no for an answer."

Lanelle shrugged her shoulders. "I can't help it if I'm good at convincing people of what's best for them, darlin'."

CHAPTER 2

There was nothing quite like being awakened by the hot breath of a big dog. Heather had slept like a rock last night, despite the cup of caffeinated coffee before bedtime. She and her mother had stayed up for a while chatting about this and that, not bringing up the subject of her running the inn again. She knew her mom was gearing up for a big conversation, so Heather's plan was to sneak out of the house early and spend some time getting reacquainted with Jubilee before she came back to face her mother.

This had always been their dynamic. Lanelle liked to have important conversations, and Heather liked to hide from them. She was much more accustomed to numbers and data. It wasn't emotional. But Lanelle was an emotional type of person. Family meant a lot to her. Heritage. Legacy. It was everything to her, and Heather didn't know how to tell her mother that she couldn't come home permanently. Maybe she could help her in the short term by giving her some business advice, but there was no way she could give up her life back in the city.

"Murphy, get out of my face!" she said, laughing as the dog leaned forward and tried to lay down on top of her. She rolled to the side, and Murphy scooted into bed right next to her. Thankfully, she wasn't allergic to dogs because now her bed was covered in white and brown hair. She had never seen a dog shed that much.

She looked over at the clock on the bedside table. It was time to face the day, and she couldn't stay in bed cuddling with Murphy any longer. As much as she wanted to spend time with her mother, first she wanted to head out into town and see some of the people and places she hadn't seen for such a long time. She knew she would have to have the conversation with her mother, but at least she could get breakfast and a cup of coffee first.

She swung her legs over the side of the bed, being

careful not to disturb Murphy who was happily snoozing already. She swore that dog did nothing but take naps. Every time she spoke to her mother on the phone or did a video chat, Murphy was nearby sleeping. His favorite place was a window upstairs where he could overlook the street in the town square. Murphy loved to people watch. He hated delivery trucks, and he especially disliked the mailman, but other than that he quietly sat all day watching everything that went on in Jubilee.

Heather quickly got dressed, putting on a pair of tan shorts, a pink T-shirt and pulling her hair into a ponytail. "I'll be right back, boy," she whispered to Murphy who looked up at her with his trusting eyes. His eyes were the color of chestnuts. "Keep my spot warm."

She headed downstairs and quickly wrote a note to her mother, leaving it on the kitchen table. She let her know that she was going out for a little while but would be home by dinnertime so they could talk. She could see Lanelle out in the backyard watering her flowers as she always did in the morning and evening.

Slipping out the front door, Heather walked up the sidewalk, hunger brewing in her stomach. Her first stop was at The Rustic Spoon. She loved to get a breakfast sandwich there, and this morning it was the Canadian bacon, egg and cheese. After picking that up, she walked over to Perky's to get her favorite cup of coffee. There was just something about the coffee at Perky's. It tasted better than any coffee on earth. Of course, it was the same old coffee everybody got. It wasn't like Jubilee was known for growing coffee beans. But in Heather's mind, it tasted better.

"Well, I do declare! I can't believe I'm seeing Heather Callaway standing here in my coffee shop!" Isobel Perkins, the owner of Perky's, came out from behind the counter and hugged her tightly.

The coffee shop had been under her ownership for at least the last twenty years, and she was very well known for being involved in everything going on in town from the Chamber of Commerce to planning the festivals. Now in her early seventies, Isobel was a little heavier than Heather remembered her, but she still looked much the same. She always kept her dyed black hair in a bun atop her head, and she always wore her favorite blue eyeshadow.

"Perky, it's so good to see you! How's Eddie?" Perky had been married to her husband for close to fifty years, and he was well known in town as the best mechanic you could possibly find. Having grown up on a farm and worked on all the equipment his whole life, there wasn't much Eddie couldn't fix.

"Oh, he's about the same as always. Always getting up to no good! Now, what are you doing in town? Lanelle didn't tell me you were coming."

"Just wanted to come for a quick visit. I think Mama wants to talk to me about taking over the inn."

Perky's eyes widened, and her face lit up. "Is there a chance you're going to do that?"

Heather shook her head. "I don't think so. I love my life in the city. I love my job. I can't ever see coming back to Jubilee full time." She said the words, but she never totally believed them.

Perky's face fell a bit. She imagined that's what her mother's face was going to look like when they had the same conversation in a few hours.

"Well, I suppose you have to do the right thing for you. I'm blessed that all my kids are here in town. Jack is on the city council. Marianne is a schoolteacher. And then there's Lorna. She's an artist. It wasn't our first choice for her, but she does a right good business at the festivals."

Heather would've ventured to say that most people stayed in Jubilee if they grew up there. It was just one of those things that was expected generation to generation. She was one of the only people she knew from her high school that had left permanently. A lot of kids went off to college and came right back to help the family business, and sometimes it made her feel selfish that she hadn't done the same.

"I'm glad to hear they are all doing well. I haven't seen Marianne in years. I hope I run into her."

Marianne and Heather had gone to school together, and they had spent quite a bit of time having fun in those days. They had even double dated for prom.

"What can I get ya this morning?"

Heather smiled broadly. "I think you already know."

Perky giggled. "You know I don't even have that on the menu anymore, right?"

"But you said you would always make it for me."

"Of course I will, darling. Anytime you decide to come home to Jubilee, I will make you your special coffee drink. Give me just a minute."

As she disappeared behind the bar to make Heather's famous latte with Irish cream and chocolate, Heather walked over and sat down at one of the tables. She looked around the room and noticed a lot of the same faces that would have been there ten or fifteen years ago. Of course, they were older, but they were all still there, loving life in Jubilee. A part of her wondered why she didn't feel the same. Why did she feel the need to run as soon as she could?

A few moments later, Perky walked around the counter and handed the drink to her, holding onto one of her hands for a moment longer. "It was so good to see you. I do hope you'll stay in town long enough for your mama to get a long visit with her only daughter."

If there was one thing the women of Jubilee were good at, it was laying the guilt on real thick. "Thanks for my drink," Heather said, winking at her. She walked toward the door, turning back to wave at Perky one more time.

MADELINE HUMMED her favorite song as she steered the golf cart down the gravel road toward the mailbox. It was way earlier in the morning than she normally checked the mail, but she realized she had forgotten yesterday. As the early morning sun painted the sky above the Blue Ridge Mountains in shades of pink and yellow, she sighed. There was just something about these mountains. Brady had certainly been right about that. Speaking of her favorite guy in town, she noticed him leaning against his fence, his face lighting up a little bit as she approached.

He pushed off the fence and walked over, a smile on his face. "Good morning, beautiful," he said. She wasn't used to a man like him. Jacob had never been overly affectionate, but maybe that was because they were never in love the way two people should've been. It was too early to call what she was experiencing with Brady love, and she definitely wasn't planning to be the first one to say it.

"Good morning. I figured you'd be over there feeding the animals by now."

"Oh, I already did that. I got a very early start this morning. It's been quite a day already."

"Oh? What happened?"

He leaned against a tree right next to the golf cart. "Let's just say that being in a cramped trailer with Jasmine and Anna presents challenges that I didn't have before."

"Challenges? Are you saying it's not easy to live in that small space with two other people? That's shocking!" Madeline said, faking surprise as she put her hand to her chest.

Brady chuckled. "You have no idea. This morning, Jasmine and I were practically dancing around each other, trying to get ready for the day. I think I bumped into her at least a dozen times. It brought back a lot of memories of our teen years when we would both be trying to get ready for school. I can't tell you how many fights were started on those mornings."

"I'm trying to imagine that in my mind. A young, handsome Brady getting ready for school or a date. I bet Jasmine could tell me some stories." Madeline had only met Jasmine in passing so far. She'd been there for a few weeks, but she didn't seem to want to interact with much of anybody yet. Madeline could only imagine that she was still going through a lot of trauma from the situation she left. She looked forward to getting to know her better.

"I bet she could. We'll make it work somehow, but I just don't want to ruin our chance of getting close again. There was a time when I would've said Jasmine was my best friend until she started making some bad decisions, leading up to her ill-fated marriage."

"It's all going to be okay. I just know it. And I'm here for you, all of you."

His eyes softened. He walked over and touched

her shoulder. "I know you are, and I appreciate it. I don't know what I would do without you, Madeline Harper."

"Well, let's not find out."

Brady leaned down and kissed her softly on the lips. "I'd better go check on Gilbert. He was acting a little ornery this morning."

Madeline laughed. "Gilbert was ornery? I can't believe it."

"See you at lunch? The Rustic Spoon is serving your favorite country fried steak today." Madeline swore she had gained ten pounds in the last few months. She wanted to feel bad about that, but all she felt was hungry.

"I'm there. Have a good day."

HEATHER'S STEPS slowed as she approached Away With Words. The bookstore had been a familiar part of her life since childhood. Clemmy, who had been her teacher in fifth grade and worked for the school system for years, had opened the store while Heather was still in middle school. She'd retired shortly after teaching Heather and opened the popular bookstore.

As she opened the door, the sound of the bell brought back so many memories. And then there was the comforting scent of old paper and leather-bound books taking her back to a time when this place was her sanctuary. Clemmy sold new and used books, separated into sections. Heather loved to read, even now, and she spent a lot of time at the bookstore as a kid and even as a high schooler.

Clemmy looked up from behind the counter, her eyes twinkling behind her cat-eye framed glasses. "Well, if it isn't Heather Callaway!" she exclaimed, running around the counter to embrace Heather. "It's been so long. I bet your mama is just tickled pink to have you home."

"It's great to see you. You look just the same, as always."

Clemmy pulled back to look at Heather. "You look beautiful as always, but I can see that something is troubling you."

Heather smiled slightly. "Is it that obvious?"

Clemmy laughed and led Heather over to the sitting area. There were two overstuffed armchairs on one side, a table in the middle stacked with coffee table books, and a long sofa on the other side. Heather loved the old furniture. It was made of velour, and the colors were less than modern. The chairs were orange, and the sofa was green.

"Honey, I've known you since you were knee high to a grasshopper, so I can always tell when something's wrong."

Heather settled into one of the plush armchairs, feeling the weight of her decision about the inn looming over her. "I came to find a good book to read in the evening, but I also think I came here to get a bit of your advice. It's always so good."

Clemmy sat down across from her, her wise eyes studying Heather's worried face. "I thought as much. So tell me what's going on."

Heather sucked in a deep breath and started to explain the situation about her mother wanting her to come take over the inn. She also explained the reluctance to leave her successful career and life in Atlanta. Uncertainty was clouding her mind.

Clemmy listened intently, occasionally nodding and expressing a thoughtful facial expression. When Heather stopped, Clemmy reached out and took her hand.

"Heather, you know I'll support you in whatever decision you make, but I think you need to ask yourself, what do you truly want? Not what your mother wants or what you think you *should* want, but what does your heart want? Do you love working and being in the city, or do you love being in Jubilee with your family and friends? Only you can decide that."

Heather's eyes welled up with tears because Clemmy's words always struck a chord with her. "I don't know. I'm so torn."

Clemmy squeezed her hand, her voice gentle. "Take your time. Explore your hometown for a little while and reconnect with people and places that shaped you and made you into who you are. And when you're ready, your answer will come. Remember, it's okay to have roots and wings."

Heather nodded her head and felt a bit of peace settling over her. She knew Clemmy was right. She needed to rediscover her hometown, see what was going on at the inn, and figure out who she was. Was she still the big city finance career-driven woman, or did she want to come home and reconnect to her roots?

They spent the next half hour browsing the shelves, with Heather selecting a few novels that she could lose herself in over the coming days. As she prepared to leave, Clemmy hugged her again, whispering, "You'll find your way, Heather. I have faith in you."

With a grateful smile, Heather stepped back out

into the city square, the sun starting to dip behind the trees. Her heart was lighter because she knew that whatever path she chose, she had the love and support of those who cared for her. In her hometown of Jubilee, she was never truly alone.

AS HEATHER WALKED the path home to the inn, she looked at the sidewalk in front of her where she had a view of the inn. It was nestled among the Blue Ridge mountains, and it stood as a comforting symbol of her family's legacy.

As it came closer into sight, a smile tugged at the corners of her mouth as a cherished memory washed over her. It was a summer evening many years ago when she was just a little girl. The sun was sinking below the horizon, casting a golden glow over the inn. The windows were open to the warm breeze and laughter filled the air as the inn's guests mingled in the garden. Her grandparents, the second generation of Callaways to run the inn, were hosting one of their famous garden parties. The tables were full of delicious Southern food, and colorful flowers filled the garden. There were twinkling fairy lights that were strung between the trees.

She remembered the sensation of her hand in her grandfather's strong grasp as he pulled her through the crowd, introducing her to all the guests with pride. Her grandmother, wearing an elegant floral summer dress, was laughing with some of the visitors, and her face was glowing with hospitality and warmth. Music was playing softly in the background, just a gentle melody that seemed to encompass the entire garden.

Heather danced with her grandfather, her tiny feet stepping on his and laughing as he twirled her around. The night went on and the guests began to go to their rooms, so Heather's grandparents took her to the porch. They sat on the swing, all three of them together, looking out at the stars. Her grandfather told stories of how the inn had first come to be, and he always spoke of those stories filled with so much pride and love. She'd fallen asleep on her grandmother's lap, lulled by the movement of the swing and the safety of her family's embrace. When she woke up, she was tucked into bed, the memory of the night's magic still fresh in her mind.

Now, as an adult, Heather gazed at the inn from afar. That memory settled deep into her heart, which was a warm reminder of the legacy that could await her if she made the decision to come home and run it. She could almost hear her grandfather's voice and feel her grandmother's gentle touch. It was very hard to say no to the opportunity to come back to Jubilee and be at the helm of the inn that had been her family's legacy for so many years.

CHAPTER 3

The dining room in the small trailer that Brady was sharing with his sister and niece was only set for three people, and it took up most of the space of the kitchen.

Ever since he watched his house burn down and had to move this trailer onto the property, he worried about how he was going to live in a house with his sister again. They had gotten along when they were younger, but as they got older and Jasmine started making some poor decisions, Brady pulled back.

But now he had a niece, and he wanted to get to know her, if nothing else. The aroma of fried chicken filled the confined space. It was a simple meal, but it felt special to finally have his family together since they'd lost their parents and grandparents years ago. Jasmine was all he had left, and now that Anna was part of the mix, he really wanted to make the adjustment process work for all of them.

Brady took his seat and watched as Jasmine served Anna some chicken and mashed potatoes. Her hands were slightly trembling. He knew she was having a hard time regaining her footing in the world because the shadows of her past were not easily shaken off.

"Jasmine, you should take a look at some of the job openings in town. Maybe you could work at Perky's or at The Rustic Spoon," he suggested, his tone casual, but obviously filled with concern.

Jasmine paused, and her eyes met his. "I appreciate your help, brother, but I really need some time to figure things out on my own for a while."

"I know," he said quickly, seeing that she was frustrated. "I just wanna make sure you're okay. That's all."

"I know you do," she said, softening a little. "But I feel like you're hovering, and I'm a grown woman. I've been through a lot, and I just need to find my own path."

He nodded understanding, but he had a hard time shaking his protective instincts. He was a

Southern gentleman of the chivalrous sort for sure. All he really wanted to do was hunt her ex down and spend a few minutes out behind the barn with him.

After they ate in silence for a few minutes, each of them lost in thought, Anna's voice broke through the quiet moment. "Mama, I'm scared about starting school here," she said, her voice trembling. "What if the kids don't like me? What if I don't have any friends or I get bullied?"

Jasmine reached across the table and took her daughter's small hand in hers. "Oh, sweetie. You'll make friends. You're a wonderful girl. And remember that Madeline even said she'd take you over to the bookstore to pick out some new books. Maybe you'll meet some kids over there. I think they do book readings for kids your age."

"I'll make sure you meet some kids before school starts," Brady interjected, smiling at Anna. "You'll be completely comfortable by the time you start school."

Anna's eyes brightened a bit, and she smiled at him, reassured by his words. The rest of the meal passed with lighter conversation, but the underlying tension remained. Jasmine was caught between being thankful for Brady's support and the desperate need for her to reclaim her independence.

After so many years, Brady could see this and was torn between wanting to be the protective big brother and respecting her independence.

As they cleared the table, Brady caught Jasmine's eye. "Just know that I'm here for you, whatever you need, whenever you need it."

"I know," she whispered, her eyes starting to well with tears. "And I'm thankful. I truly am. I want to feel like myself again, but I'm not even sure what that is."

He pulled her into a comforting embrace, feeling the weight of her struggles and wishing that he could take them away altogether.

Anna was at the sink washing her dish off and humming a song, her worries momentarily forgotten.

HEATHER'S HEART swelled with affection as she walked up onto the front porch of the inn. She could smell the home-cooked food wafting through the air as her mother opened the front door with a smile.

"There's my girl," she said, pulling Heather into another huge hug. They settled into the dining room, and Heather was so happy at the sight of the spread of Southern comfort food that awaited her. Meatloaf, collard greens, cornbread, and Lanelle's famous peach cobbler were all lovingly prepared and displayed on her grandmother's china.

"Mom, this looks so amazing," Heather said, her mouth watering at the sight.

Lanelle smiled with her eyes crinkling at the corners. She really was getting older, but she was still just so beautiful. Heather had long wished she looked like her mother. Instead, she looked like a female version of her father. He was a handsome man, but Heather wished she had her mother's blue eyes and blond hair instead of her boring light brown hair.

"Nothing but the best for my girl, especially since you don't visit that often. Now, let's enjoy all this food."

As they dug into their meals, the conversation flowed naturally, but then it turned to the subject that had been weighing heavily on both their minds.

"Heather, dear, I can't tell you how much it means to have you home," Lanelle began. Her voice was soft, but full of emotion. "The inn has been in our family for generations, and I just want nothing more for you than to be the one who carries on our legacy."

Heather looked at her mother sensing there was more to this request than what she was letting on.

"Mama, I know how much this inn means to you, but I have a life in Atlanta. I have a whole career there. I have friends. I have my apartment. I can't shake the feeling that you're not telling me everything."

Lanelle's eyes flicked away for just a moment, a hint of something hidden in their depths.

"I just want my daughter around. Heather, you're all the family I have left."

Heather reached across the table and took her mother's hand.

"I love you, Mama, and I want to be here for you, but this is a huge decision for me. I need to know everything that's going on before I can make this kind of choice."

Lanelle squeezed Heather's hand, a small smile on her lips.

"I understand, honey. Just take your time. We'll talk more about it, I promise."

As they continued to eat, the conversation shifted to lighter topics such as all the gossip around town, but that unspoken question still lingered in the air. When they were finishing up their meal, the doorbell rang, the soft chime of it echoing through the inn. Lanelle rose, wiping her hands on a napkin.

"That must be our new guest."

Heather didn't know there was going to be a new guest. She assumed that the inn was going to be empty while she visited. She didn't know how busy it was these days, after all. Heather followed her mother to the front door, her curiosity piqued. When Lanelle opened the door, a tall stranger stood in the threshold. He had warm eyes. He was very handsome, and Heather felt a flush run up her face.

"Good evening, ma'am. I'm Ethan. I have a reservation to stay here for the next few days."

"Yes, Ethan, I'm so happy to have you. Come on in. Welcome to All Tucked Inn. So what are you doing in Jubilee?"

"Well, I'm a historian and a writer. I'm traveling through the Blue Ridge mountain towns for a new book. Jubilee happens to be my last stop before I head back home to Texas." He had a thick Southern accent, but it was a bit different from what she heard from the locals of Jubilee.

"Well, we're glad to have you here. Let me take you upstairs and show you to your room. Oh, I'm being very rude. This is my daughter, Heather. She's visiting from Atlanta."

Heather's eyes met Ethan's with a spark of connection passing between them. There was something about him, something intriguing. As Lanelle showed Ethan to his room, Heather lingered in the hallway with her mind whirling with emotions. The evening had brought more questions than answers, and suddenly the appearance of this handsome stranger was adding another layer of complexity to her already turbulent thoughts. Handsome men tended to do that to her.

She looked out the window watching as the sun dipped behind the horizon, casting a darkness over Jubilee. The town was always calling to her, beckoning her to stay, but her path was less than clear to her. With a sigh, she went back to the dining room and started cleaning up. The future of the inn, her relationship with her mother, and the mysterious allure of that handsome stranger upstairs all awaited her. She knew that her journey in Jubilee, on this visit anyway, was just beginning.

HEATHER'S MIND was way too restless to get any sleep. The quiet of the night seemed to just increase her thoughts, and the weight of her mother's request pressed so heavily on her heart. She was finally unable to bear the silence in her room, so she slipped out of the bed and walked down the hallway as quietly as possible.

The soft glow of the front porch light beckoned her, so she went outside hoping the cool night air might help her clear her head. But to her surprise, she found Ethan sitting in one of the front porch rocking chairs with a notebook in his lap.

He looked up as she approached, a smile lighting up his eyes. "You couldn't sleep either?"

She returned his smile, feeling an unexpected ease in his presence. "No, not at all. What are you doing up?"

"Just writing," he said, closing his notebook and setting it aside. "The night often inspires me. Sometimes the busyness of the day gets in the way of my thoughts. So when it's quiet and dark, I don't have much else to do but write."

She chuckled. "Or you could sleep."

Ethan nodded his head. "I suppose you're right, although I've never been great at it."

Heather took a seat in the other rocking chair next to him, intrigued by this stranger who had suddenly become a part of her world. "So tell me about your writing. What kind of historian are you?"

He leaned back, his eyes taking on a faraway look. "I specialize in local histories, the stories of small towns and the people who built them. There's just something so magical about uncovering all the hidden layers of a place and discovering the connections that binds the community together."

"That sounds fascinating. So what brought you to Jubilee specifically?”

"Jubilee's history is rich and captivating," he explained. "There's this blend of cultural influences from the legacy of the Callaway family to the Native Americans who lived here first. The very soul of this place has a certain magic to it, so I wanted to explore it and to understand what makes Jubilee so special."

As they talked, Heather found herself drawn into his world, fascinated by the insights and the way he saw things. She had lived in Jubilee for much of her life, and she had never thought of it the way that he did. She started to ask more questions about his travels, his research, and his life in Texas. He answered her with an openness that surprised her as he painted vivid word pictures about his experiences. The conversation flowed, and she found herself confiding in him a bit, talking about her own struggles with the decision that was weighing so heavily on her.

"My mother wants me to come back and help at the inn. I love this place, but I just don't know if I'm ready to give up my life in Atlanta. But then my mother's getting older, and I know she needs my help. I'm her only child and the only living relative that could take this place over."

He looked at her, his eyes filled with understanding. "It's a difficult decision, I'm sure, but sometimes the path that we're meant to take reveals itself in such unexpected ways." Finally, Ethan stood up, stretching his long limbs. "I should probably try to get some sleep. I've got a lot of research to do tomorrow. I'm hoping your mother can help me with some of that."

"I'm sure she will," Heather replied. "And thanks for listening." He looked back at her before walking in the front door.

"Goodnight, Heather. It was a pleasure talking to you."

As he retreated into the house, Heather sat on the front porch, her heart racing a bit. It had been a long time since a man had been interesting to her, and this one was certainly that. Not only interesting, but highly handsome. But then she knew he was only there for a brief time, and for all she knew he was married and had twenty-four kids back at some house in Texas. So she tried to push the thought away. With a sigh, she headed back to her own room, still thinking about the decision and conversations that were to come with her mother.

THE FIRST HINTS of dawn were beginning to stretch across the sky over the mountains, casting a soft pink glow over Brady's farm. He quietly flipped pancakes on the griddle while his sister slept in the other room.

The scent of sizzling sausage filled the air, and he hummed a song to himself feeling happy in the pleasure of just cooking breakfast for his little eight-year-old niece. Anna, who was still rubbing her eyes from sleep, stumbled into the kitchen, her hair a tangled mess of curls. Her face lit up at the sight of the pancakes. Brady scooped her up in a big hug, laughing at her sleepy grin.

"Good morning, sweetie. Ready for some pancakes?" She nodded, eagerly running to a chair at the kitchen table, her eyes staring at the griddle.

"Yes. Are we going to feed the horses today?"

"You bet," Brady said, flipping a pancake onto her

plate and giving her a generous helping of sausage before dousing everything in syrup.

"Don't forget about Gilbert. That crazy goat would be mighty upset if we left him out." Anna's giggle rang through the kitchen. Brady felt a warm swell of affection for the little girl who had so quickly become a part of his heart. She had been through so much in her short life, but her spirit was unbreakable.

They ate while chatting about different things at the farm, savoring the meal in the quiet of the early morning. Anna was finished and pushed her plate away, her eyes wide and serious, "I like it here, Uncle Brady. I feel safe."

Brady reached across the table and squeezed her tiny hand. "I'm glad, and you are safe. You're always going to be taken care of Anna. You never have to worry about that."

She smiled, but her eyes always held a little hint of sadness. "I miss my daddy though, even though he did some bad things."

Brady's heart ached for her. He knew how confusing that must be to a little girl. She loved her father, but her entire life had been spent watching abuse happen right in front of her. It was probably going to take a lot of therapy over the years to get her to a place of understanding.

"It's okay to miss him. Remember, we are here for you, and we love you." She ran over and hugged him tightly. With a smile, he wiped away a few tears rolling down her cheeks and then held out his hand. "Come on, let's go feed those horses now."

Hand in hand they walked toward the barn. The sun was now fully risen in the sky, which cast a golden glow over the fields. The horses nickered a greeting and Gilbert, the mischievous goat, bleated loudly from his pen demanding their attention.

The morning air was crisp and filled with a pleasant earthy scent of the farm. As Brady and Anna made their way to the stables, the horses were very eager for breakfast, stomping their hooves and tossing their heads when they recognized the familiar sounds of the feed buckets. Brady handed Anna a small scoop and showed her how to measure the grain. Her eyes were wide with wonder as she looked up at the tall gentle animals. There was just something about the way they moved with the power and grace that seemed to resonate with her.

"They are mighty good creatures," Brady told her, "but you know they need love and care just like people do." He showed her how to pour the feed into the troughs. She followed his direction, her face glowing with pride every time she did it.

"I think this one likes me," she said, pointing to a brown mare that had nuzzled her hand.

Brady could see they had a connection forming, and he made a note in his head to take her for a ride on the horse as soon as he could. Trust and understanding often grew between horses and humans. "Oh, that's Bella," Brady explained reaching out to pet the mare's velvety nose. "She's got a kind heart just like you. She's been through some things, but she's strong and determined."

Anna reached out a hand timidly to pet Bella. The horse blew softly and gently bumped her head against Anna's hand. "See, you're a natural," Brady encouraged. They continued down the line feeding each horse, and Anna grew more and more confident. She talked to them, told them about school that was starting soon and about her favorite books. Brady thought he even heard her say something about her daddy to one of them.

It was hard for him to hear how much she missed her father, given what he had done. Brady wanted to go after him with his bare hands, but he knew if he did something like that, then Jasmine and Anna would be alone.

Finally, they reached the pen that was holding Gilbert, Brady's mischievous and ever-hungry goat. His eyes were bright and ambitious as he scrambled toward them. His bleat was demanding and insistent. "Well, it looks like somebody's ready for breakfast," Brady said chuckling.

He gave Anna a handful of hay. Gilbert practically inhaled the food, his beard twitching as he chewed. Anna laughed, delighting in his antics. Gilbert was like a one-man comedy show. "He's so funny," she said, reaching out to scratch behind his ears. Of course, Gilbert leaned right into it. His eyes half-closed with pleasure.

"He sure is," Brady agreed, "But he's as stubborn as a mule and can be a handful sometimes, kind of like somebody else I know."

Anna stuck out her tongue, and Brady laughed, tousling her hair. The sun was climbing higher now, and it was time to get on with the day. But Brady had enjoyed his morning just spending time with the animals and his precious new niece that he was blessed to get to know even though she came to him in turbulent circumstances. They finished the chores, Anna chattering away about this and that before heading back to the house.

CHAPTER 4

Morning came way too early for Heather. She got up, sat on the edge of the bed and stared out the window over the Blue Ridge Mountains. She would never get tired of looking at that view, but it was still really early, given that she got no sleep last night.

She did enjoy her chat on the porch with Ethan, but she really wished she could have gotten more hours of sleep before having to get up. She couldn't continue sleeping because there was light pouring through the window and she could smell her mother's delicious breakfast cooking downstairs. So she got herself dressed, pulled her hair into a ponytail and slowly walked down the stairs, still rubbing the sleep from her eyes. She could hear the bacon crackling and smell her mother's homemade biscuits. She didn't know what else she had in store for her, but she was starving, so anything was good. As she walked into the kitchen, she saw her mother standing there wearing her familiar apron.

She'd had the apron since Heather was a kid, and she didn't know how it wasn't torn apart and in tatters by now. It had little cherries all over it, and Heather often wondered where she got it. Maybe it was a gift from Heather's father or something passed down from her grandmother. She'd have to ask one day.

"What are you cooking that smells so good?" she asked before sitting down at the breakfast table and putting her head in her hands.

"Biscuits, bacon. I've got some hash browns cooking over here, scrambled eggs..." Heather rolled her eyes and laughed.

"Are you cooking for an army?"

"Well, I figure Ethan's going to need breakfast and you'd be pretty hungry. I know you haven't been eating much in the city, probably a bunch of salads." Lanelle was not a fan of the city. She thought that Heather should come home and live a good, quiet Southern country life in the mountains while gorging herself on chicken and dumplings and fried pies.

Heather wasn't so sure about that, but she did love the food. "Well, it smells great and no, I haven't been eating a bunch of salads. Have you seen how much weight I've put on?"

"Oh, please dear. You're as tiny as you've ever been," Lanelle said, rolling her eyes and laughing. She made Heather a plate and walked over, putting it on the table in front of her. "Coffee?"

"Of course. I need the caffeine." Lanelle poured her a cup of coffee and set it in front of her with cream and sugar just as Ethan was coming down the stairs.

"Good morning," he said smiling. He was wearing a pair of jeans and a tight-fitting gray T-shirt. Heather struggled not to let her face turn red looking at him. He wasn't exactly Southern looking, even though he lived in Texas, but he also didn't look like he came from the city. He just looked handsome. That was pretty much it.

"Good morning, Ethan. I hope you'll join us for breakfast," Lanelle said.

"I would love that. I've been enjoying a lot of Southern cooking as I've traveled around. It's been a struggle to keep the weight off," he said laughing.

Heather wanted to tell him he looked just fine, but she refrained. It had been a long time since she'd been on a date and that was really starting to show.

"Care for some coffee?"

"Of course, thank you. Black." He sat down next to Heather at the table. "Did you end up getting any sleep?"

"Just a little," she said. Her mother eyed her carefully from across the kitchen. She made Ethan a plate and took it over to the table before making hers and sitting down with them.

"So what are your plans today, Ethan?"

"Well, I need to go out into the community and get some information for the book. Maybe spend a few hours at the courthouse looking over old records."

"How long do you think you'll be here?"

"I'm hoping for no more than a week or two, but as long as it takes, really."

"And then you're heading back to Texas?" Lanelle asked, as if she was interrogating him at the police station.

"Yes, ma'am. Time to get back home and put this book together."

"Are you married, Ethan?" Heather shot her

mother a look like she wanted to crawl under the table.

"No, I'm not. Divorced, actually, about ten years ago."

"Oh, I'm so sorry."

Heather always wondered whether that was a good thing or a bad thing. If he hadn't ever been married at his age, there might be something really wrong with him. But since he had and was divorced, she wondered why the divorce happened. Was it his fault? Was he a cheater? Her mind was running away with her. She really needed to get some food in her stomach so she started eating in an effort to keep her mouth full.

"So tell me more about this place, if you don't mind. It would really help me with my history."

Heather laughed. "Oh, no. You've opened the floodgates now. Mama will be glad to tell you everything you ever wanted to know about this town."

"Why don't we start with the inn? I love the name All Tucked Inn. That's adorable. Who named it?" Lanelle took a few bites of food and then swallowed some coffee before speaking.

"Well, the first generation was Eliza and James Callaway. They owned this place in the late eighteen-hundreds, so they were the original founders.

They purchased a large property here in the heart of Jubilee, and they built the inn as a place for travelers, miners and loggers to rest. James was a very skilled craftsman, but Eliza had a flare for hospitality, much like I do. So they worked to create this welcoming environment, and the inn quickly gained a reputation for its warmth and charm. People would come from miles around to stay here. They had three children, two sons and a daughter, and the entire family was involved in running the inn."

"Wow, that's wonderful that you have so much information."

Heather looked at Ethan and smiled, "I told you. She's just getting started."

Lanelle continued, "The second generation owned the inn in the early to mid nineteen-hundreds, and that was Oliver Callaway. He was the eldest son of Eliza and James, and he took over the inn. He expanded it, adding more rooms and the dining area. This became a popular destination for tourists who were exploring the Blue Ridge Mountains during the Jazz Age. I love to think back to that time and wonder what it would've been like to be here. Well, anyway, Oliver married a local woman named Amelia. Now Amelia was the one who introduced a lot of herbal remedies and local dishes to the inn, using the recipes handed down through her family. There's a friend of mine named Geneva that's in that lineage, and she still practices herbalism today."

"Really? That's interesting. Maybe I could meet with her. I'd love to learn more about what she does."

"Of course, I can arrange that. Geneva loves to talk. She also does a lot of wildlife hikes and shows people the local herbs and medicinal plants in the area. She's very smart about that stuff, so I'm sure she would love to meet with you."

"Wonderful. I appreciate that. Sorry, I didn't mean to interrupt you."

"Oliver and Amelia had two daughters. One daughter, Victoria, was the one who showed a particular interest in the inn and the traditions. So the third generation was Victoria. She ran it in the mid to late nineteen-hundreds. She took over the reins from her father and continued the legacy. She upgraded the inn a little bit by adding some modern amenities but preserved its original architecture. She was known for hosting literary meetings, art exhibitions, and even local festivals. This inn was a cultural hub during that time. She married a musician named Henry, and they had one daughter named Lanelle," she said, smiling at Ethan.

"So that was your mom and dad. Very interesting that they were so cultural."

"Oh, Ethan. Don't think that just because we live in the mountains that we're a bunch of hillbillies. We have culture here, too."

"I'm sorry. I didn't mean to offend. So, what was it like growing up at the inn?"

"I loved it. I wouldn't have had it any other way. I was a part of the daily life and running of this place from a very young age, and I've been running it for years. After the death of my mother, I became the matriarch of All Tucked Inn. I've seen some economic ups and downs, and it's been a challenge keeping this place alive. We've done some things like wellness retreats and nature tours, partnering with Geneva, trying to keep up with the modern trends. I married a businessman who worked in Atlanta, and I had to convince him that we needed to stay in Jubilee. So for many, many years he drove back-and-forth for hours each day just so I could keep my family's legacy."

"And you're the only child, Heather?" he asked.

"Yes, they tried to have more, but I'm all that God provided," she said laughing.

"So as you can see, the history and legacy here is very rich and we're intertwined with the growth and culture of Jubilee. This place is still the go-to spot for hikers starting on the Appalachian Trail. We'd like to get more people to come stay here and experience how wonderful Jubilee and the Blue Ridge Mountains are."

"I can see why, if for nothing else other than the food," Ethan said laughing.

MADELINE WALKED into the bookstore just before lunch, deciding that she needed to look for a new craft book; not that she did crafts, but the craft of writing. She felt like she never learned enough, and she always wanted to better herself even all these years later.

The soft rustle of people turning pages in books and the faint scent of coffee filled the air as she walked in the door. Just as she rounded the corner to look for her book, her eyes fell on a familiar face. She was surprised to see Jasmine standing there.

"Jasmine?" Madeline said approaching her.

Jasmine looked very absorbed in whatever she was looking at in the self-help section. She looked up, her eyes momentarily clouded with confusion before she realized who was talking to her. "Oh, Madeline. Hi."

"What brings you here?" Madeline asked, looking down at the book that Jasmine was holding. It was a guide to dealing with grief and trauma. Her stomach clenched.

"I, um, I was just looking for something to read," Jasmine stammered, her face flushing.

Madeline could see that her hands were shaking. Her gaze softened, understanding. There was unspoken pain behind Jasmine's words. She gestured toward the nearby sitting area. "Do you want to sit down and chat for a bit?"

Jasmine's eyes lit up at the offer. They walked over and sat down in the two plush chairs surrounded by shelves that were filled with all kinds of books. "I didn't expect to run into anybody I knew," Jasmine began, holding onto the book in her hands to the point where her fingers were starting to turn white.

"Me neither," Madeline admitted, "but I'm glad I did. How have you been settling in? I really haven't seen you around as much as I've seen Anna." Jasmine's smile fell. She looked down, her voice barely above a whisper.

"It's been really tough. Brady is a wonderful

brother, but he's always hovering over me, watching me. I feel like I'm on display. I know he means well, but he's suffocating me. I want to find a job, but honestly, my anxiety just skyrockets every time I think about even going to an interview or working someplace where I have to deal with the public. I just feel stuck. I need to do something. I have a daughter to raise, and I can't stay with my brother forever. The space is so small that we're stepping on each other all the time."

Madeline just allowed her to speak and get it all out because she had probably been bottling it up for quite some time. She reached over and gently placed her hand on Jasmine's.

"I cannot pretend to understand exactly how you feel, but I've been through my share of troubles, not like yours. Nothing even close to that, but my husband did cheat on me with my best friend. I walked in on them, and it left me feeling shattered and betrayed, but it also left me alone running my business. They both worked for me."

Her eyes widened at the revelation, "I had no idea. You seem to have everything together. Brady just adores you."

“Nobody has it all together, no matter how much they want people to think that,” Madeline said with a small smile. "We all have our own battles, and I adore your brother, too, but I was thinking that maybe you and I can help each other out."

Jasmine looked at her, "How do you mean?"

"Well, I could use an assistant to help handle my social media, respond to emails, that sort of thing. It's something you could do from home at your own pace. What do you think?" Jasmine's face lit up, hope blossoming in her eyes.

"Really? You would trust me with that."

"Of course, I would. I'm sure Brady would vouch for you. I know you want to get a fresh start. I see strength in you and you remind me a lot of some of my strongest characters. So even if you don't see that strength in yourself, just know that I do."

Tears welled in Jasmine's eyes. She suddenly reached out and pulled Madeline into a tight hug.

"Thank you. Thank you so much."

"You can come to my house for some training, but you can work at the trailer as much as you want."

Jasmine chuckled. "Honestly, I need to get out of there sometimes, so if it's just the same to you, I might work from your house most of the time."

Madeline nodded. "That works just fine."

They spent the next hour chatting, sharing their stories and fears and dreams. Two women, both wounded by life in different ways, finding a connection in each other's company. Madeline was so happy that she was bonding with Jasmine because she hoped that her relationship with Brady would be permanent. That would mean Jasmine was family, too. When they finally parted, Madeline going to get some lunch and Jasmine heading back to the farm, the friendship they had forged in empathy was a bond that would see each of them through any storms yet to come.

THE SMELL of chicken and dumplings filled the air in Madeline's cozy kitchen as she placed the finishing touches on the meal. She was so excited to have Brady and Geneva over for dinner tonight. She invited Jasmine, but Jasmine wanted to take her daughter out for pizza just as a way to spend some bonding time as mother and daughter. Geneva, her next-door neighbor and now close friend, was helping set the table, and Brady was finishing up making the sweet tea for the three of them.

"You're really doing a great job decorating the place. I like that new bear picture over the fireplace," Brady said.

"I just can't help myself. I keep buying everything with bears on it. I know it's kind of kitschy, but what are you supposed to do when you live in the mountains?"

He laughed as they all walked over and made their plates before sitting down at the table.

"I heard Heather's back in town," Geneva said. "Have you seen her, Brady? You knew her when y'all were kids, didn't you?"

Brady's fork paused in midair. "Yeah, I did. She was a few years younger than me, but I do remember her well. She was a sweet girl. I heard she's back to help her mom at the inn. I guess I should go see them soon."

Madeline smiled. "I'd like to meet her. I've heard good things about her. Clemmy is very close to Heather from what I understand."

Their conversation shifted quickly to Jasmine and Anna. Brady's expression turned more serious. "Jasmine is really having a hard time adjusting. She loves being at the farm, I think, but the close quarters are getting to all of us. I'll be so glad when I can get my house rebuilt. Anna is also nervous about starting at a new school."

"That's understandable," Madeline said. "I can see being that age and not knowing what to expect. As for the house, do you have your plans all drawn up now?"

"I do. It's just a matter of waiting for the builder to get started. They're going to clear the land and start with the foundation soon. I think that will help a lot when we're not all on top of each other in that little trailer."

"So I understand that Jasmine has been having some trouble adjusting," Madeline said, not making eye contact. She finally smiled slightly and looked up at Brady. "I offered her a job as my assistant. That way she can work from home and get back in the swing of things at her own pace. Plus, she can start putting some money away."

Brady's eyes widened. A mixture of surprise and concern. "Really? I mean that's generous of you, Madeline, but are you sure? What if things don't go well? I don't want you to blame me if..."

Madeline reached across the table, placing a reassuring hand on his arm. "I trust Jasmine, and I trust you. I believe in giving people chances, and she definitely needs a second chance. A lot of what has happened to her and Anna was not Jasmine's fault. Yes, she made some bad decisions in her life, but we all do that."

"You're very understanding," Brady said, reaching over and holding her hand.

"And don't worry, I won't hold you responsible if things don't go perfectly." He looked into her eyes and nodded.

"Okay, I believe you and thank you for doing this for her. I think it's really going to help."

They continued to eat, the conversation meandering through all kinds of memories that Geneva had and experiences Brady shared. Geneva talked about some of her most recent nature hikes and a class that she was going to be teaching at the courthouse about local plant life.

They laughed just like they did every time they shared a meal together. The strong bonds that Madeline had formed with Geneva and Brady in such a short few months was amazing to her. She was closer to them than she had been to some of her lifelong friends back in the city. She would always cherish the fact that she had these two wonderful people in her life.

As the evening wore on and the dishes were cleared, they lingered over cups of coffee and pieces of pound cake. Madeline hadn't made that. She had stopped by the bakery and picked it up earlier. She did make the chicken and dumplings from a recipe she found online. She was working hard at getting better and better with her Southern cooking.

"You know, it's so good to have you all here," Madeline said. "It just reminds me that no matter what changes we have in our lives, some things always remain the same. Family, friends, the simple joy of sharing a meal together."

Each of them smiled and raised their cup of coffee, toasting each other. Madeline had never been happier in her life. She felt like moving to Jubilee had given her the new beginning she didn't know she needed.

CHAPTER 5

The little town of Jubilee was abuzz with activity. As Heather walked down the bustling main street to the other side of the square, she made her way toward the farmer's market. Her thoughts were preoccupied with the inn and her mother and how she was going to work this whole thing out. She'd been getting calls all morning from the office even though she was supposed to be on somewhat of a vacation, and her email was full of questions and problems that she had to handle. It was very hard to do it all while also trying to figure out how to help her mom even though she didn't even really understand what all the problems were.

As she made her way down the street, a familiar face caught her eye. She saw Ethan, who was sitting at an outdoor table at Perky's. He seemed engrossed in his notebook, his hand moving quickly across the page as a cup of steaming coffee sat beside him. Heather approached, and he looked up. A warm smile spread across his face. "Heather," he called waving her over. "Care to join me?" She felt a pleasant flutter in her stomach as she walked over to him. There was just something about this guy that drew her in. He seemed kind and genuine.

"Hey, Ethan," she said, taking the seat across from him. "What are you up to today?"

"Oh, I'm just jotting down some more notes. I went over to the courthouse and spent some time looking through the files the last couple of days." He closed his notebook. "I like to really immerse myself in the places that I write about. Perky's definitely has a certain charm. Every town I go to has its own personality, but I have to say that Jubilee is one of my favorites. It just feels like home even if it's not your home."

"That's a really great way to think about it." It did feel like home. It *was* her home. It would always be her home even if she chose to live somewhere else. "I'm on my way to the farmers market. I just need to get some fresh ingredients for dinner tonight. I think Mama wants to make a big side salad because she's expecting some new guests, and we're going to need some more food."

They sat for a few moments chatting, talking about Jubilee, some of Ethan's travels and the different places he'd been. Heather found herself drawn into his stories. He was a great storyteller, and the thought occurred to her that maybe he should write fiction novels, too.

Eventually, the conversation started to shift to more personal matters. Ethan's eyes took on a distant look when he mentioned his life back in Texas. "So you told my mom that you're divorced. I hate to pry, but I kind of want to know what happened." Heather felt terrible when the sentence came out of her mouth. What kind of person asks someone that kind of question when they barely know them?

"I guess it was just one of those marriages that didn't work out. We were only married for four years. We grew apart. The divorce was tough. I suppose you could say we just fell out of love. She was my high school sweetheart and, you know, you change a lot when you get older."

"Divorce is never easy. I mean, I've never been married, but I know a lot of people who have divorced, and it's always tough. There were no kids?"

"No kids. She went on to get remarried, and she has two kids now. I'm happy for her about that, and there's still time for me, I guess."

"So you want kids?" Her stomach started to flutter a bit. Heather had always wanted kids, but she had just never met the right man.

"I do want kids. If God wills it, then it'll happen. Biological or adoption. Either way is fine with me. I'd love to share some kind of legacy with my kids. I'm a little jealous of you, to be honest."

"Jealous of me? Why?"

"Well, you have a great relationship with your mother, for one thing. I don't have that. My mother wasn't the best, unfortunately. But more than that, you have this amazing history in your family. The legacy of the inn is just kind of... romantic. Wow. That sounded really nerdy and not manly at all," he said, laughing.

"Not nerdy at all! I guess I'd never thought of how cool knowing our family history really is."

"I wish I had something like that to pass down to my own kids. I don't know much about my family history."

"Well, there's always time to learn."

"I suppose you're right."

They continued to talk, conversation flowing

naturally. Heather found herself wanting to share more about her own life, her own dreams, her fears and the pressures of taking over the inn. Before she knew it, over an hour had passed, and his coffee had to have been cold.

"I'm so sorry to have kept you here so long. I'm sure you have other things to do and I need to get to the farmers market before they close." They both stood up and stayed there for just a moment looking at each other.

"I've gone to a lot of towns and I've never met a friend, but I consider you to be a new friend," Ethan said.

"I consider you to be a friend, too. I'm glad you came to Jubilee, Ethan. I'll see you tonight at dinner." She watched him walk toward the inn, and she turned to head toward the farmers market. “Hey, Ethan? Wait!”

He turned around. “Everything okay?”

“Yes. It’s just that I have a friend named Geneva. I think my mom mentioned her to you. She's very knowledgeable about the town and all sorts of things dealing with the local wildlife and herbal stuff. Would you like to go meet her?"

"Oh, but I thought you needed to go to the farmers market."

"Well, if you don't mind, we can run by there real quick, and then we can just head straight over to Geneva's. I'll text her right now."

"That would be wonderful. Thank you so much."

THE SUN WAS BEGINNING to slide behind the mountains, which was casting a golden hue over the landscape as Heather drove Ethan toward Geneva's house. She loved those moments when there were just enough clouds for streams of the fading light to peek through like spotlights on the mountains below.

Geneva knew just about everything about Jubilee's traditions and stories. She was the unofficial keeper of the history of the town, and, when you visited with her, it was like stepping into the heart of the town itself.

Heather could tell that Ethan was excited to get to meet Geneva. As they pulled down the gravel road toward her tiny cabin, the woods were thick and green and wildflowers grew on the edges of the road. It had rained recently, and Heather could see all different colors of mushrooms springing up in the forest. She loved this place and the aura of timelessness it had.

They pulled into Geneva's driveway, and Heather turned to give him a warning. "Geneva is quirky and unique. I just want you to know that. She's probably wearing something very colorful, and her wild hair is always all over the place. She looks the part of the town historian."

Ethan laughed. "This place is incredible," he said, looking out the window. "This forest looks like something from a storybook."

"Well, it is the national forest, so it stays protected, but, yes, it's a beautiful place. It always feels so mysterious to me, and I think that's why Geneva is full of stories about it. There are all kinds of local legends in this area aside from Bigfoot, which is the well-known one."

He laughed. "Her cabin is adorable. It's also quite eclectic. Inside she has a little of everything, and she's probably going to send you home with some tincture or essential oil, so just be ready."

"I'm not worried," Ethan said laughing. "This is exactly the kind of thing a historian lives for."

They got out of the car and headed up to the front porch where Geneva was waiting. She smiled and introduced herself. "Hi, you must be Ethan. I'm so glad to have you here."

"Thank you so much for welcoming me into your home."

"Heather, my darling," she exclaimed when she saw Heather behind him.

"Geneva, it's always good to see you."

"Come in, come in," Geneva said, ushering them inside. "I've got some sweet tea, and I've made some fresh-baked oatmeal raisin cookies. I hope you like them, Ethan."

"Of course. Thank you so much, ma'am."

"Oh, please stop calling me ma'am. It makes me feel older than I am, even though every morning when I get up, and hear my joints creak, I feel pretty old." Ethan and Heather laughed.

They settled into Geneva's cozy living room surrounded by old photographs and antique furniture and all of her various collections. Heather could smell the scent of some herb or tincture off in the corner where she had a bunch of them lined up.

Geneva had always been a captivating storyteller, weaving tales of the town's founding, the legends of the mountains and the stories of the native wildlife and plants. The entire time Ethan was enthralled, his notebook filling up with details and insights.

Heather watched him, taking pleasure in seeing his interest in their town. She knew that Geneva's stories were going to add to the depth of his book and help him understand the true soul of Jubilee.

One particular legend caught Ethan's attention, which was a tale about a hidden waterfall in the mountains where lovers would go to make eternal promises. "The water is said to be enchanted," Geneva explained. "Those who drink from it together are bound by love forever." Ethan looked up, his eyes wide.

"That's beautiful. It's like a fairy tale."

"It's part of who we are," Heather added. "These legends, these stories, they shape our community. They connect us to each other and to our past."

They spent several hours with Geneva, time slipping away as it became dark outside. She realized that her mother was going to be worried, so she sent her a quick text to let her know that she would be home soon.

As they drove back toward the inn, Heather couldn't help but feel deeply satisfied. She had shared something special with Ethan, something that was unique to Jubilee. She felt their bond deepening and even if it was only friendship, she was happy to have him around. It had been a long time since she'd had someone to truly confide in. He was no longer a stranger to her. He was becoming part of Jubilee and part of her life, and now she wondered if both of them were going to have a hard time leaving when it was time to go.

MADELINE LOOKED OUT HER WINDOW, smiling as she saw Anna skipping toward her porch. The eight-year-old's ponytail was bouncing with each step. Brady had dropped Anna off for an afternoon of fun and bonding while he took Jasmine into town for some grocery shopping. Sometimes a mother just needed a break. Madeline was looking forward to spending quality time with the little girl who she was starting to see as family. Anna bounded up the porch steps, her eyes sparkling with excitement.

"Hi, Ms. Madeline," she called out.

"Well, hello, sweet Anna," she replied, opening the door and bending down to hug Anna. "You ready for an afternoon of fun?" Her eyes widened, and she nodded.

"Yes, please."

Madeline took Anna into the living room where

she had set up a whole crafting table filled with paints, paper, glitter, and other fun supplies. Madeline had never had children of her own, so she knew she would enjoy this time with the little girl. They started painting pictures and making cards, laughing at each other's messy hands, and Anna began to open up to Madeline, talking about her fears going to a new school. She said she was having lots of fun living with her Uncle Brady on the farm. Madeline listened attentively to every word because she felt like this child may not have been listened to a lot in recent years. Of course, Jasmine had done her best given the situation.

"Do you want to take a break?"

"Yes. I think I need a break," Anna said, pretending to be exhausted.

"I thought we might bake some chocolate chip cookies together." Anna's eyes danced with delight.

"That would be so fun."

They went over to the kitchen and started mixing the dough before placing spoonfuls of the concoction on the baking tray.

As the cookies baked, they sat at the kitchen table, drinking milk and talking.

"Miss Madeline," Anna said hesitantly, "do you think my mommy's going to be okay? She seems to be really sad, and I've tried to make her happy, but I don't know what else to do."

Madeline reached across the table and took Anna's small hand. "Oh, sweetie, your mommy is going through a tough time but she's strong. She's going to be fine. She has you and Uncle Brady to support her and me, too. She'll get better, I promise, but it's not your job to make her happy, you know?"

"I know, but I just want to help her. She's always helped me."

"You're helping her by just being you. Okay?"

"Okay. I told Uncle Brady that I miss my daddy sometimes, even though he was mean to my mom. Do you think that's wrong?"

"No, Anna," Madeline said. "It's not wrong to miss someone you love, even if they did things that weren't very nice. It's okay to have your feelings. That is always okay."

They sat like that for a little while, Madeline comforting Anna and letting her express her fears and confusion. She was going to talk to Brady about getting Anna some therapy just to make sure she could work out these emotions that she had brought up to both Brady and Madeline at different times.

When the timer finally dinged to announce that the cookies were ready, Anna's mood lifted immediately, and she was excited to taste their delicious creation. The rest of the afternoon passed with a joyful blur of cookie eating, more crafting, dancing to music, and watching Anna's favorite TV shows. By the time Brady came to pick her up, Anna was bubbling with happiness and high on sugar. That was the great thing about kids. They seemed to bounce back from terrible situations so quickly.

"Thanks for watching her today," Brady said, as Anna ran past them out into the yard to play with one of the wind chimes that hung on a shepherd's hook in the garden.

"She's a wonderful little girl, but I think she's struggling. It might be time to get her someone to talk to." Brady nodded.

"Already on it. I talked to her pediatrician today, and they gave me a referral."

"That's great. I think she'll be fine, but she just really needs to get these emotions out and learn how to cope with them."

"Thanks again, Madeline. I know she enjoyed spending the day with you." He walked closer and kissed her softly on the lips. "I promise we'll have some time alone soon. I know things got crazy when my sister and niece got here."

She shook her head. "I wouldn't have it any other

way. I love being a part of your family, so you don't need to worry about me."

As she watched him walk away and head down the gravel road holding Anna's hand, Madeline felt a sense of gratitude she'd never felt before in her life. God had really blessed her when he forced her to come to Jubilee.

LANELLE STOOD in the lobby of All Tucked Inn, a warm and welcoming smile on her face. She always loved to receive new guests, and Heather could tell that this time was no different. The aroma of freshly baked peanut butter cookies filled the air as the door opened and a young family entered. They were excited to be there, which just excited Lanelle further.

"Welcome to All Tucked Inn," Lanelle said, sticking out her hand. "I'm Lanelle, and I'll be your host during your stay. This is my daughter, Heather. She helps me here at the inn." It wasn't lost on Heather that she said that, but she didn't correct her.

"You must be the Lancasters."

"That's right. I'm Dawson. This is my wife Julie, and this is our son and little adventurer, Dylan." He pointed towards a boy who looked to be about eleven or twelve years old.

"It's my pleasure to have you here," Lanelle said. "I hear this is Dylan's first hiking trip."

"Yes. We live in Seagrove, South Carolina, on the coast. So Dylan has never seen the mountains, and he's certainly never gone on a nature hike," Julie said, smiling as she put her arm around her son. She was obviously very proud of him.

"Are you excited about this, Dylan?"

"Absolutely. I want to climb a mountain and see a waterfall. And I want to..."

"Slow down, buddy. We're going to get to as much as we can, but we're only here for the week-end," Dawson said, laughing.

"Well, we have some wonderful trails around here, perfect for a young explorer like yourself."

Julie smiled appreciatively. "We're thrilled to be here. Seagrove is beautiful, but we wanted Dylan to experience the mountains. So can you recommend any local sites for us to see while we're here?"

"Of course," Lanelle said. She reached for a brochure on a nearby counter. "Well, we have the Willow Creek Trail, which is perfect for families and not too steep. It leads to a beautiful waterfall. And then there's Bears Den Overlook, which gives you a beautiful overlook of the Blue Ridge Mountains. If you want a bit of history, you can also visit the Jubilee Mountain Museum or even go to our courthouse on the square. There is a small museum there as well."

Dawson's eyes lit up with interest. "I love anything historical. They all sound amazing. We'll definitely check them out. Thank you, Lanelle."

She handed them their keys and escorted them up to their room, describing the inn's amenities, as well as what time breakfast and dinner were along the way. They settled into their cozy room, which was filled with antique furniture and framed pictures of the Blue Ridge Mountains.

"If you need anything at all, don't hesitate to ask me or Heather," she said, pointing to her daughter. "And don't forget to try our peanut butter cookies we just made. We will have breakfast at seven AM sharp in the morning."

"Thank you for making us feel so welcome," Julie said. "We run an inn ourselves, and I know just how hard that can be. Sometimes you just don't feel like having people in your house."

Lanelle laughed, "This inn has been in our family for four generations, and sometimes I am a bit tired, but I love having new guests."

Heather watched her mother carefully. She did seem tired, but she was getting older and Heather didn't know how much of that was just age.

"Enjoy your evening, and just let me know if you need anything." She closed the door behind her, looking like she had a sense of fulfillment on her face. Heather knew her mother loved running the inn, but the fact that she had called her there for help meant that something was definitely wrong, and Heather intended to find out what it was.

CHAPTER 6

Heather held the phone up to her ear. "Yes, I know, I know. I don't remember what that final number was. I'm going to have to look through my computer files." She had been on the phone for the last half hour with one of her coworkers. They were trying to find a spreadsheet, and they couldn't locate it on the main computer. Heather knew she had a copy of it on her personal computer, but that was upstairs, and she really didn't want to walk all the way up there. "Just give me the name of the client and the account number." As she looked around the kitchen, she couldn't find a piece of paper or a pen, so she walked over to the small office that Lanelle kept under the stairs. "Hang on, hang on. I have to find a piece of paper." She looked on the desk, which was a mess, as it had always been, and she finally found a small piece of paper. She grabbed a pen from the cup and wrote it down. "Okay, repeat it one more time. Got it. I'll call you back in a few minutes."

She ended the call and absentmindedly started shuffling through the stacks of paper on the office desk, trying to figure out how to get it organized. Over the years, she had done this a million times, even as a teenager, but Lanelle always made a mess of it again. She said it was her own organized chaos, but nobody else would have any clue what any of it meant. Heather couldn't say anything; her desk looked much the same.

She was lost in thought, thinking about Ethan more than she should have been, when she noticed something unusual among the paperwork. "What is this?" she murmured to herself, pulling out a statement that looked out of place. Her years in the finance industry meant that she could look at a stack of papers and immediately see if something was wrong.

Her brows furrowed as she started to examine the financial documents. The numbers didn't make sense. The more she looked, the more she found entries of unpaid bills, dwindling savings, and increasing expenses staring back at her. She started hearing alarm bells in her head.

Her mother had always been meticulous about the finances, even if her desk was a mess. These figures pointed to something very troubling.

"Heather?" Lanelle's voice echoed through the corridor, momentarily breaking the concentration she had.

"Coming," Heather called back, her eyes still glued to the papers. She set them down and quickly left the office, closing the door behind her. Feeling a prickle of worry, she walked upstairs to her mother's room where she was laying down on the bed, Murphy snuggled up right beside her. She looked unusually pale, and her eyes didn't have their normal sparkle. "Mama, is everything okay?" Heather asked, concern dripping from her voice. Her mom forced a smile, but her voice was weaker than normal.

"I'm just a bit tired, dear. Nothing to worry about. I just wanted to tell you that I made some chicken salad earlier if you want it for lunch."

Heather's instincts told her something was terribly wrong. The paperwork, her mother's appearance and the unspoken tension in the air all pointed to something more serious. "I wanted to talk to you about the inn."

"Oh, honey, I'm so tired. I just need a quick nap. Can we talk about it later?" It was very odd that Lanelle had wanted to talk about this the whole time and, now that Heather brought it up, she was not able to speak about it. Something had to be wrong.

"Of course. Just let me know when you're up later and if you need anything, you can call me on my cell phone. I'll be around here."

"Okay, honey. Thank you. I'm fine. Everything is okay. I promise."

Heather quietly closed the door, and walked down the hallway, and back downstairs where she found Ethan standing in the foyer.

"Is everything okay? I thought I heard you yelling."

"Oh, my mom called to me. I went upstairs, and she was laying down. She didn't look right. And I..."

"What?"

"Nevermind. You're a guest here. I shouldn't be unloading on you." She walked toward the kitchen and sat down at the breakfast table.

"I thought we decided we were friends."

"Well, we are."

"Okay, then don't friends talk to each other?"

"Yes, I suppose you're right. Something's going on with my mother. She wants me to run the inn, but she hasn't said why. I know she's getting older, but she just seems so worried about it, wanting me to come home as quickly as possible."

"Did you ask her?"

"Many times. And then just now I tried to bring up the subject, but she told me she was too tired and needed to take a nap. You don't know my mom, but she's very energetic. Always has been. She didn't look right."

"Do you think maybe you should call the doctor?"

She thought for a moment. "No. I feel like she already knows what's wrong. She's just not telling me. And then I just went in the office, and I found some things that are very concerning."

"Like what?"

"Financial papers. It seems like my mom is in trouble financially, like maybe the inn is in trouble. I just don't know what to do."

"It seems like all you can do is wait for her to feel a little better so you can talk."

"I don't know if she's going to be honest with me, and I have to find out what's going on. I can't go back to the city not knowing. If there's something medically wrong with my mom or the inn is about to go under, I have to do something about it."

"But what do you think you can do?"

"I don't know. I'm in the finance industry, so I should be able to figure this out. Do you mind watching the stairs for a moment just in case she comes back down? I need to go gather some paperwork in the office so that I can look over it."

"Of course. I'll watch."

Heather ran over to the office and quickly went through all the piles she found on the desk, taking the papers that she needed to look at. "I'm just going to go put these up in my room and hide them."

"Okay. If there's anything else I can do, please let me know."

"I will. Thanks for listening, Ethan. It means more than you know."

HEATHER SAT in her favorite corner booth at The Rustic Spoon, her eyebrows furrowed as she pored over the papers strewn across the table. The financial records from All Tucked Inn were like a maze revealing all kinds of twists and turns she didn't even know existed.

There were repair costs, loan agreements, and overdue bills that painted a picture she had not expected when she came home to visit. She hadn't even taken a bite of her grilled cheese sandwich because she was so absorbed in the numbers. She was trying to figure out what it all meant. The door chimed and Clemmy walked in, a warm smile on her face as always. Sarah, one of the servers, greeted her with a wave and went to get her to-go order.

"Heather, mind if I join you?" Clemmy asked.

"Of course not. Please, sit." Heather tried to hide the papers, but she knew that was futile. Clemmy was as sharp as a tack, and she noticed them immediately.

"What's all this then?" Clemmy asked, her curiosity piqued. She settled into the booth and put her forearms on the table, looking down at the papers. Heather sighed, feeling the weight of the world on her shoulders.

"It's the inn. Mama's been dealing with some major repairs, and I found all of these loans that she's apparently taken out."

Clemmy's eyes softened. "Oh, Lanelle's been having a hard time of it lately. You know, these short-term rentals have been stealing business left and right. Folks don't see the charm in the old ways like they used to."

Heather's eyes widened. "Short-term rentals? Here in Jubilee?"

"Oh, yes, my dear. Cabins, cottages, even rooms in people's houses. They're cheaper and the younger crowd seems to like them better. Your mom's been fighting for the last few years to try to keep up."

"I had no idea." Heather's heart ached at the thought of her mother struggling with all of this alone. How had she not noticed that something was wrong? How had she not thought about the fact that short-term rentals might be taking business away from their inn?

Clemmy reached across the table and took Heather's hand. "Your mama's strong, Heather, and now she has you here, and I'm sure together y'all will figure this out." They sat in silence for a few moments, the chatter in the diner a soothing sound in the background.

"Thanks, Clemmy. I needed to hear that."

Clemmy squeezed her hand. "Well, I've got to go. My food's going to get cold. But just remember, you've got the heart of this town inside of you, Heather. You'll find a way." With a final smile, Clemmy got her order and left, walking down the sidewalk towards the bookstore, but she left Heather with a renewed determination. She would find a way for her mother, for the inn that meant so much to their family, and for herself. There were answers out there. She just had to look.

HEATHER'S HEART was pounding as she approached the inn. This was the day, and this was the time that she was going to find out exactly what was going on. One thing that the conversation with Clemmy had left her determined to do was talk to her mother and figure out exactly what was wrong with her health and what was going on with the finances. She was anxious about their upcoming conversation. She didn't want to talk about her mother's financial struggles, her tiredness, all the loans, but she needed answers and she needed them now if she was going to have any chance of helping.

She found Lanelle in one of the guest rooms, dusting the furniture. Her face was a bit pale and her movements were slower than usual. Maybe some of that was just a result of Heather having been gone for so many years. She just hadn't noticed how her mother was aging, so it was much more jarring and shocking to see her now.

"Mama," Heather called softly, concern etched in her voice.

Lanelle looked up, forcing a smile. "Heather, honey, I didn't hear you come in." Murphy wagged his tail, and Heather reached down to scratch the top of his head.

"You should not be doing this," Heather said, her voice firm, although she didn't know who else would do it. They didn't have a housekeeper or any other staff. Lanelle had always done everything herself, and she seemed like superwoman to Heather for so many years. Now, she was starting to show some cracks in that armor.

"You're overtired, Mama."

Lanelle waved her hand dismissively. "I'm fine, dear. I'm just a little worn out is all."

Heather's patience was wearing thin. "No, Mama, you're not fine. I found the loans, the bills. I see how tired you are. What in the world is going on? Why didn't you tell me that you were struggling?"

Lanelle's face fell, her mask of strength crumbling into a million pieces. "I didn't want to worry you," she whispered. She sank down onto the edge of the bed and Heather sat beside her.

"I'm here now. You don't have to do everything alone, but you have to tell me what's happening. You have to be honest."

Tears welled up in Lanelle's eyes as she looked

away. "The inn has been struggling, Heather. Competition, repairs, and then there's my health."

"Your health?" Heather's heart clenched with fear. She was about to hear things that she didn't want to hear. It was a turning point in her mind, that moment when a parent becomes elderly. That moment when health conditions start to take over and slowly pull them away. Maybe she was being overly dramatic or negative, but she was scared.

Lanelle took a deep breath, her voice quivering a bit. "I've been diagnosed with atrial fibrillation. It's a heart condition, but it's not usually life-threatening. I'm just having to take some medications, and it's been making me incredibly tired."

"Why didn't you tell me? I would've come home sooner."

Lanelle shook her head, tears rolling down her cheeks. "I didn't want to force you. I wanted you to come home because you wanted to, not because you felt obligated. I feel so guilty asking for your help. People live with this condition every day. I should be able to continue handling everything."

"Mama, you're not a superhero. I've always thought of you as one, but that's not realistic. You're a person. You can only take so much."

"Well, I couldn't hire anybody because of our

financial situation, so the only thing I knew to do in the end was call you, or shut the doors and put a for sale sign out front."

Heather pulled her mom into a big hug. "I want to be here. I want to help. You're not alone anymore, and we'll figure this out together."

Lanelle's body shook with quiet sobs as she clung to her daughter. "I'm so sorry, Heather. I just didn't know what else to do."

"We'll find a way. I promise we'll find a way." Even as she said the words, Heather didn't know what that way would be. She didn't know how they were going to find a way, but she'd made a promise to her mother, and she intended to keep it.

As they sat together, mother and daughter, the weight of the challenges ahead settled on Heather's shoulders, but she knew with absolute certainty they would face them together like they had done everything else. She could weather the storm when her mother couldn't. The inn, their family legacy, would survive. She would make sure of it.

THE MORNING SUN was just starting to peek over the mountains as Dawson, Julie and their son Dylan hurried about in their room at All Tucked Inn. There was excitement buzzing through the air because today was the first hiking trip they were taking as a family. It was an adventure into the unknown and a shared family memory.

Dylan had never been on a hike before in his life, and Dawson and Julie weren't exactly experienced. Having lived in Seagrove, South Carolina, for a long time now, Dawson was used to the ocean, he was used to the marshes, but he definitely was not used to the mountains. He spread out a map of the local trails across the bed. His eyes scanning up and down the different paths, calculating distances and assessing how challenging each trail would be. He had a sparkle in his eyes that Julie hadn't seen in a long time.

"I think this is the right trail," Dawson said, pointing to a marked path. It led to a waterfall, which was something that Dylan definitely wanted to see. "It's not too long, and I think Dylan is going to love this waterfall at the end."

Dylan's eyes widened. "Really? A waterfall? Do you think we'll be able to swim in it?"

Dawson laughed, ruffling his son's hair. "I don't know. We'll see, buddy. It might be a bit cold, but we can definitely dip our feet into it."

Julie watched them, a mixture of joy and apprehension in her heart. They'd never done anything like this before, but Dawson was confident. He was always sure of himself. He was a strong head of their family, and she trusted him.

Yet, the worry lingered. "You've got everything planned out, right?" she asked, unable to keep the concern out of her voice. "We've never hiked before and this trail..."

Dawson looked up, and his face softened as he walked over and took her hand. "We'll be fine, Julie. I've researched, I've planned and we've got everything that we need. We'll just take it slow, we'll enjoy the day and we'll keep each other safe."

Julie searched his eyes looking for reassurance and found it. She always did. His smile was warm, his touch steady. She nodded. "What about bears?"

"There aren't going to be any bears. I've done all kinds of research on the area, and even if there are bears, I have this bear spray in the backpack. It's going to be okay."

Julie smiled. "Okay, let's do this."

Together, they packed up their backpacks with food, water, first aid supplies, and extra clothing. Dawson double-checked their hiking boots, making sure they were sturdy and well-fitted. A few minutes later, they were loading up the truck, the mountain air fresh and invigorating as it filled their lungs.

Dylan was almost bouncing in his seat. He was so energetic this morning, which was unusual for a boy his age. But he was getting to do something fun today, something he had never done, and it made Julie feel proud that they were able to take him on this trip.

"Are you ready for an adventure?" Dawson asked, looking back at his son as he started the engine.

"I'm ready," Dylan cheered, his smile wide.

Julie looked at Dawson, and her worry was now replaced with anticipation. They were going to do this. They were going to take a hike out in the woods together as a family, these beach people, these non-forest people, and even though she was still a little worried, she was more excited.

HEATHER AND ETHAN strolled through the local park. Jubilee had one of the most beautiful parks Heather had ever seen. Not only did it have playgrounds and some ball fields on one side, but it had beautiful hiking trails right next to the river, and she loved to go there when she was home.

They walked through the park, the sound of laughter from nearby children filling the air. As they approached the lake, Ethan stopped to look at a historical marker. His eyes widened with interest. "Did you know there was a battle fought here during the Civil War?" he asked, his voice filled with curiosity.

Heather glanced at the marker and then back at him. "I did, but I don't know all the details. It's strange to grow up in a place and still not really know that much about it. There's always something to learn. I guess I took it for granted when I was a kid."

Ethan nodded. "History is like that. It's full of all these hidden layers. Just when you think you've uncovered everything, you find something new."

"You mean like with people?"

Ethan smiled. "Exactly like people."

They continued their walk, the conversation flowing effortlessly. Heather talked more about her time away from Jubilee, about her work, her dreams, her ambitions. She also talked about the complicated emotions tied to returning home. Ethan was a good listener. He listened intently, occasionally sharing his own experiences about life on the road, his passion for history that started when he was very young, and his longing for a place to call home.

As they reached a secluded spot by the lake, Heather sat on a bench, her eyes fixed on the water. "I feel like I'm at a crossroads. I have to decide between the life I thought I wanted and the responsibilities that I have here."

Ethan sat down beside her. "What do you want, Heather?"

She sat there for a moment, thinking as she stared at the water. "You know, I don't know anymore. I thought I had it all figured out. I thought my life was all set, but now everything has changed. With my mother's health and the inn's financial trouble, I just feel like I'm losing control. I feel like if I don't step up and do something, we could lose the four generations of legacy from that inn, and that would all be on my shoulders."

"That would not be your fault, Heather. A lot of things have happened that you couldn't control and didn't know about."

"Yes, but I can probably fix all of it if I really put my mind to it."

"You know, sometimes losing control is the first step toward finding the right path. Maybe this is an opportunity and not a burden."

She looked at him, a glimmer of hope in her eyes. "You really believe that?"

"I do. I've seen it in my own life. When my marriage ended, I felt lost, but it led me to a new understanding of myself and what I truly wanted. Maybe this is your chance to discover what's truly important to you."

"Thank you. I don't know what I would do without my new friend. I like to talk to others in town that have known me forever, but I have to say they might be a little biased. They love my mother and the inn, and they want it to stay." They sat there for a long time, these two people brought together by circumstance, but forging a connection that went beyond mere acquaintances.

CHAPTER 7

Dawson, Julie, and young Dylan had been hiking for hours. The crunch of the leaves underfoot and their laughter filled the forest. The trail had led them throughout the lush forests, over gurgling streams, and finally to that waterfall they had so eagerly anticipated. It was a majestic cascade and a sight to behold. They'd spent a whole hour just enjoying the view and chatting. Dylan had run around at the foot of the waterfall, the cold mountain water shocking him at first. He had even stood under the waterfall itself, letting it spray down on his head.

As the day wore on and they started to hike back, the sense of adventure was still high, but then the sun began to dip, casting long shadows through the trees. Julie felt her stomach start twisting with anxiety.

"Dawson, are you sure we're on the right path?"

He looked around, his brow furrowed

"I think so. I mean, it looks familiar."

Julie thought that everything looked familiar. They were in a forest, and all the trees looked pretty much alike.

Dylan, skipping up ahead, turned around with a smile. "Dad, when can I play with my video games?"

Dawson laughed. "Once we're back at the inn, buddy."

Julie's concern deepened when she suddenly realized something.

"Dawson, did you bring the bag with the phones and the map?"

His face turned pale, his eyes wide. "I thought you had it."

She shook her head. "No, I had the food and water. I thought Dylan's bag had the phones."

They both turned to Dylan, who was frowning at his backpack.

"I switched bags at the inn. I wanted the bigger one for my games and my books."

A chill ran down Julie's spine, and panic began to

set in as the gravity of their situation hit her square in the head.

They were lost in the wilderness, in the mountains without phones or a map. Dawson was obviously trying to remain calm. He kept his voice steady.

"It's all right. We just need to retrace our steps. I'm sure that we can find our way back."

Hours passed as they stumbled along unfamiliar paths, the woods growing dark and foreboding. Fear and frustration mounted as every turn seemed to lead them further from where they needed to go. Dylan's laugh had started to turn into tears, and Julie's anxiety had turned into dread. Here they were, out in the middle of the national forest, and this might be where they died. She was terrified. It got darker and darker.

Finally, Dawson stopped, his voice breaking a bit. "I don't know where we are. We're lost."

Those words hung in the air as the terrible reality settled over them. Dylan was obviously scared, but Julie was petrified. They were stranded in the wilderness with no way to call for help, and they had no idea how to find their way back. This adventure they had so eagerly anticipated had become a real nightmare, and now they were faced with the scary prospect of spending the night in the forest - cold, hungry, and completely lost. In the fading light, they huddled together, a family united by love, getting ready to face a long and uncertain night. The forest, which had been a place of beauty and wonder just a few hours ago, was now a maze of shadows and fear.

MADELINE AND BRADY sat at The Buzzed Bear, the warm glow of string lights giving it a welcome ambiance as the evening settled over Jubilee. They were sitting in their favorite corner booth, the soft murmur of other people talking providing a pleasant background hum. They held hands atop the wooden table, fingers laced together as if they had always been meant to fit together. "You're really doing something wonderful for Jasmine," Brady said. "I can't tell you how much it means to her and to me."

Madeline smiled. "She's been through so much Brady, and if I can help her find her footing again, I'm more than happy to do it. I can't wait for us to start working together tomorrow morning."

"You have a heart of gold, Madeline. That's one of the many things I adore about you."

A blush crept up her cheeks as she looked

down. "I could say the same thing about you. You've been so supportive of your sister and your niece, taking them in and helping them start over. It's inspiring."

"Well, it's family. You do whatever you can for family, right?"

"And for those you love," Madeline added, looking at him. Their gazes locked, an unspoken connection passing between them. They had not said the word love yet, even though it had been a couple of months that they had been dating. So much had gone on with Brady's house burning down and his sister and niece coming back. There just hadn't been a lot of time to think about where their relationship was going.

She looked at him again. "I do love you, Brady." Her voice was trembling, not from just the sincerity of what she was saying, but from the fear that maybe he didn't feel the same way. Madeline had never said she loved someone first, and honestly she didn't plan to do it this time.

His face softened. "And I love you, Madeline. I never thought I'd find someone like you. You've brought so much joy into my life that I didn't even know I was missing."

"You love me?" she said, smiling broadly.

"I thought you knew that," he said, rubbing his thumb across her cheek.

"With my recent track record, I never assume anything."

He looked at her, a serious expression on his face, and his eyes locked on hers. "Well, I do love you, Madeline Harper. You never have to question that." He leaned in and kissed her softly.

They sat there talking and chatting, and Madeline felt such a wave of relief to know that he felt the same way she did. It was hard putting her heart out there again after what had happened in her marriage. But the one person that she had thought would never let her down was Brady. And now she knew that he felt the same way about her that she did about him.

JASMINE ARRIVED EARLY at Madeline's house ready to start work for the day. Madeline could tell that she was a bundle of nerves mixed with excitement. The sun was just beginning to fill the room with a soft, golden light.

"Good morning, Jasmine, I'm so glad you're here. I can't wait for us to get started."

"Good morning, Madeline," Jasmine replied, her voice betraying her nervousness. "I'm looking forward to working with you. I just hope I can keep up."

Madeline placed a reassuring hand on her shoulder. "Don't you worry about that. You're here because I believe in you, and I know you'll do great. So let's start by getting you acquainted with everything."

Madeline spent the next half hour or so showing Jasmine around her office, explaining the various parts of her business from handling social media to responding to emails and organizing events.

Madeline was looking forward to doing more book signing events in the coming year. She had taken the last several months off after her divorce and moving to Jubilee. But she really needed to get back to work to promote her new small town series. She had already finished book one and submitted it to the publisher. She was just waiting to hear back from the editors about what changes needed to be made.

Jasmine seemed amazed by the scope of Madeline's work, feeling both inspired and slightly overwhelmed, it seemed.

"Now, here is your desk." Madeline showed her a

neatly organized space where she had put a vase of fresh flowers. "I hoped that these might brighten your first day." Jasmine's eyes welled with tears.

"Thank you, Madeline. That was so thoughtful of you. It's been years since I've had a real job, and I've never had one like this. Usually, I had to work in restaurants or retail stores."

"You're a part of my team now. I want you to feel at home here."

The rest of the day was a whirlwind of activity. Madeline threw all kinds of things at Jasmine, and she seemed to handle each one with ease. She dived into her tasks, learned the ropes, and seemed to be finding her rhythm very quickly.

Madeline tried to be patient and supportive, but there was really nothing she had to complain about. She just sat there offering to answer questions or give guidance. When they broke for lunch, they enjoyed some sandwiches and salads from The Rustic Spoon that Madeline had picked up the day before. They chatted about everything from Madeline's books to their shared love of Jubilee.

"I really can't thank you enough for this opportunity. I have been feeling so scattered like I didn't know what to do with my life. When you're in a situation like I was for so many years, your self-confidence sort of takes a beating. It just means a lot to me because everything has been so upside down."

"I believe in second chances, Jasmine, and especially for somebody like you. You might have made some choices in your past that led to undesirable places, but that doesn't mean that you can't still do great things with your life."

The afternoon was filled with more learning, more growth, and Madeline thought Jasmine seemed to be getting a newfound confidence already. The anxiety that she had arrived with was replaced by somebody who was focused and determined in her work. When the day drew to a close, Madeline and Jasmine sat down with glasses of sweet tea and reflected on the day's work.

"You did an amazing job today. I knew you would. And the way that you scheduled out the social media posts and the new graphics you made, those were things I never would've thought of."

"Thank you. I feel like I'm finally finding my way."

They sat there and talked more about what they would do the next day, and Madeline found herself looking forward to her business again. Somehow hiring Jasmine had reinvigorated her in the process, and now she looked at Jasmine not just as a coworker, but as a friend and possibly a future member of her own family.

HEATHER SAT in a booth at Perky's, her mind buzzing with thoughts and concerns over the inn's financial struggles. Geneva and Clemmy had offered to meet her there so that they could all use their collective wisdom to try to find a way to turn things around. She smelled the sweet aroma of the freshly brewed coffee in the air, mingling with the scent of warm pastries and her stomach growled. She would have to eat lunch early. Her phone rang, breaking her out of her cravings.

"Mama, is everything okay?"

"Yes, dear. Everything is fine. At least I think so."

"What do you mean?"

"Well, I noticed that that family that checked in went on a hike yesterday and didn't come home."

"What do you mean they didn't come home?"

"They never came back from their hike. Well, maybe they decided to camp in the woods."

"I didn't see a tent. Do you have their phone number?"

"Yes, of course. I've tried calling. I finally went up

to their room and realized they have a bag on the bed, and that's where the phone was ringing."

"Oh, no. That doesn't sound good."

"No, it doesn't. I hate to be an alarmist, though. Maybe they just decided to spend the night in the woods and I'll see them today."

"Maybe so. I would give it a few hours, but if they don't arrive before dinner, we need to call the authorities."

"Should I call them now?"

"I wouldn't think so. Again, they could be people who just decided to stay in the woods overnight. That happens sometimes, right?"

"Occasionally. I'll just keep an eye out for them and like you say, if they don't come back before dinnertime, I'll call the sheriff and see if we can get a search party together."

Heather looked up and saw Geneva arriving. She didn't want her mother to know that she was brainstorming with two of her best friends.

"I need to go now and do a bit of work, but I'll be back after lunch."

"Okay, I'll see you then."

She pressed end on the call just as Geneva was walking up to the table.

"Oh, darling, you look like you've been carrying

the weight of the world on your shoulders. Let's see what we can do to lighten the load."

She sat down just as Clemmy hurried in moments later, her vivacious energy a stark contrast to Geneva's motherly calm forest-woman demeanor. She greeted them both with hugs before they settled into the booth.

"Okay, let's get down to business," Clemmy said. "We've got a fine inn to save, and I reckon between the three of us we're going to be able to figure this out."

Heather felt a surge of gratitude and security as she looked at these two wise women in front of her. They each represented a different facet of Jubilee's community. Geneva, the herbalist, forest hiking matriarch. And Clemmy, the smart, sassy, trendy bookstore owner. Their insights would be invaluable.

"I've been thinking about doing events," Heather began. "We have beautiful grounds around the inn. We could host weddings, parties or even corporate retreats. It could be a new revenue stream."

Geneva nodded. "That's a splendid idea, Heather. The inn has always had a certain charm that would lend itself well to such occasions. I've mentioned it to your mother in the past and she had never wanted to do that, but I'm sure she'd be open to it now. You could offer packages that included catering, decorations, maybe even some local entertainment."

Clemmy's face lit up with excitement. "What about themed weekends, like cooking classes with a local chef or art retreats with artists from the area? Even more nature workshops led by our very own Geneva."

Geneva blushed at the mention of her name but smiled about the idea. "That could be fantastic. We could collaborate with all kinds of local businesses and create something that benefits everybody. Even the whole town of Jubilee."

The conversation flowed, ideas building upon ideas with each woman contributing a unique perspective. They talked about promoting All Tucked Inn on social media, partnering with travel agencies and offering special discounts for locals who just wanted a little getaway.

The hours passed, and Heather's notebook filled up with possibilities. Her heart swelled with gratitude for the support and creativity of these two women. When they wrapped up their meeting with promises to implement these plans, Heather felt a new sense of purpose.

"Thank you, both of you," she said. "I don't know what I would do without you."

Geneva reached over and squeezed her hand. "We're always here for you, dear. Always."

Clemmy smiled. Her eyes welling. "You know that's what family does, Heather. We stick together, come rain or shine, and everybody who lives in Jubilee is one big family."

With renewed hope and determination, she left Perky's, heading back toward the inn to help her mother. She loved having the wisdom, support and love of her community. It was something she didn't know she had been missing all these years. Back in the city, she had friends, but she didn't have this.

HEATHER ARRIVED BACK at the inn just at the same time as Ethan. She didn't know where he had been all day, probably doing some sort of research at the courthouse again. Her heart was much lighter now that she'd had her conversation with Clemmy and Geneva. The day had been fruitful, filled with brainstorming and planning, and now she felt a renewed sense of hope about the future of the inn. Having Ethan's support and friendship had also become a comfort to her. She felt very connected to him, which was weird because she didn't normally connect to people that easily.

"Mama, we're home," Heather called out as they walked in, but the unusual hum of activity was absent. Something felt weird. Lanelle appeared from the kitchen, her face a bit pale and her eyes wide with worry.

"Heather, they haven't come back."

"Who hasn't come back?" she asked.

"The Lancasters. Dawson, Julie, and their little boy, Dylan. I told you they went hiking yesterday, and they should have been back by now. Even if they spent the night, surely they would've come back today."

A chill ran down Heather's spine. She had completely forgotten about the conversation she'd had with her mother earlier. The forest was a beautiful place, but it was unforgiving, especially for people who didn't know much about it. A wrong turn could lead to disaster.

Heather nodded, her mind racing. They needed to act fast because these people definitely needed help. She picked up the phone and dialed the sheriff's office, explaining the situation with urgency in her voice. The sheriff said they would be on their way, so Heather hung up.

"We need Geneva. She knows about the forest better than anyone."

"I can go get her," Ethan volunteered.

"That would be super helpful. I'll text her and tell her to get ready," Heather said. Geneva didn't like to drive the mountain roads at night, so Ethan picking her up was definitely the best move.

As Heather and Lanelle waited for Ethan to go pick up Geneva and for the sheriff to arrive, the space filled with anxiety. As time seemed to stretch, each tick of the clock reminded them about this lost family. Surely they had to be terrified, and it was becoming nightfall again. They were going to be cold. They didn't have a tent. They couldn't have that much food and water. Heather didn't know them at all, but she felt very responsible for some reason.

About twenty minutes later, the door popped open and Geneva hurried inside, Ethan close behind her. Her face was etched with concern, but her eyes were sharp and alert.

"So what do you know about their plans?" she asked, wasting no time. Time was definitely of the essence.

"I know they wanted to hike to a waterfall,"

Lanelle said. "That's all I know. Dawson seemed really confident. He had maps and guides."

"But no guide with them," Geneva muttered, her eyebrows furrowing. "We need to gather a search party. Do you know what map he was looking at?"

"I don't know. Maybe I can find something up in their room," Lanelle said.

"I'll go," Heather said, running up the stairs faster than her mother could possibly move.

She looked through their bags, finding their cell phones, and then over on the other end of the bed, she finally saw a map. There was a red mark around one of the waterfalls that Heather was familiar with. She ran back downstairs.

"I've called Brady. He's bringing Madeline, too," Lanelle said. "They'll be here soon, and the sheriff is on his way."

"I found a map," Heather said, holding her hand up as she ran into the kitchen.

The inn started to turn into a hub of activity, transformed from a haven of relaxation to a command center. They spread the map out on the table, looked at all the trails Dawson had marked and analyzed them. They gathered up supplies like flashlights, ropes, and first aid kits. By the time Brady and Madeline arrived, the sheriff was also pulling up. Everybody was concerned because they knew just how dangerous the mountain forests could be. If somebody didn't know the terrain, one little slip and somebody could get really hurt. That didn't include the fears about bears, bobcats, the temperature and going without food or water.

"The entire town will help if they need to," Brady said. "We'll find them."

"I know we will," Heather replied. "We have to."

The sheriff walked over to the table, his uniform crisp and his demeanor authoritative. He took charge, organizing the search party and dividing the forest into sectors. Even though they were planning to go to that waterfall, it didn't mean that that's where they still were. They could have gotten quite off course, so they would start there and fan out. Geneva's knowledge of the forest was invaluable, her insights guiding their efforts. Even the sheriff didn't know the forest like Geneva did. Brady and Ethan volunteered to lead teams because each of them felt comfortable in the forest setting.

"We'll search all night long if we have to. We have to find them before the weather turns," the sheriff said.

Heather hadn't even thought about the weather, so she quickly pulled up an app on her phone. A big thunderstorm was set to roll in early in the morning. They had to get them out before then.

Heather felt a sudden surge of gratitude for the surrounding community. Watching the people of Jubilee come together in a time of crisis was something she had seen several times when she was young. It was just what they did.

"I'll take care of the inn. You go out there and help find them," Lanelle said, crossing her arms. "Here, Brady. Take Murphy. He'll lead you to them. I just know it."

Brady reached out and took Murphy's leash, the dog happily wagging his tail, ready for an adventure.

Just before the search party headed out, Anna, who had shown up with Jasmine, walked over to Brady and handed him a stuffed bear that she had bought at the department store that day.

"Can you give this to Dylan when you find him? He might be scared, and a teddy bear usually helps me when I'm scared."

"But Anna, you bought this today so you could feel better at nighttime when you have bad dreams," Brady said, putting his hand on her shoulder.

"I know, but I don't need it. Dylan needs it more than I do."

CHAPTER 8

The search through the dense forest in the dark was tiring. Heather and Ethan walked together, their conversation turning to their pasts as Heather felt herself drawn to Ethan's deep comforting Texas drawl.

"My father and I hiked this trail every summer," she said, the memories flooding her mind like they hadn't in a long time. "He showed me how to build a shelter, how to find water, how to read the stars. We would camp out, tell stories, and just enjoy being together."

"Tell me more. What's your favorite memory?"

"Boy, you really are a writer, aren't you?" she said, laughing. "Okay, let me think. I remember once we got caught in a rainstorm. This forest is an actual rainforest. Not a lot of people know that. Anyway, we huddled together in our makeshift shelter. He told me all kinds of stories about when he was young and what his dreams were. Back then, he wanted to be a boat captain, which I found really funny since he had never lived near the water."

"That is funny," Ethan said chuckling.

"He also talked a lot about his love for my mother. They had a wonderful love affair for so many years until he passed away. I don't ever expect her to even date again because she was just so head over heels in love with my dad. I think she transferred that love to the inn."

"Maybe so."

"Do you think people only get one true love?"

"I don't know. I hate to think that way because when you lose somebody, you need to be able to move on and still have love in your life. But I also believe in soulmates."

"I struggle with that idea," Ethan said. "Like what if you miss that one person that you're supposed to be with? Does that mean you're just alone the rest of your life?"

Heather laughed. "I don't know all the answers. I just know that my dad always made me feel like I could do anything, like I could be anyone."

Ethan's own memories were no less vivid. Growing up on a farm in Texas was a world away from this. "All the land was flat, the sky was huge, my days were filled with chores and animals and the warmth of family, but I always felt like I was meant for something else, like something more. That's what made me become a writer and start traveling around, and that's what brought me to Jubilee. The more time I spend here, the more I really don't want to leave."

"You don't?"

"Right now, I can't imagine it. I love this community. I mean, just the way that everybody has come together tonight is unlike anything I've ever seen."

"I'm sure a lot of small towns are this way. Everybody pitching in to take care of each other."

"No. I've been to a lot of small towns. Some of them are great. Don't get me wrong. Quaint. Nice people. But this town feels more like everybody's one big family. I don't think I've ever seen that before."

"So do you think you're going to stay?"

"I don't know. Like you, I have a home back in Texas. I have family and friends. There's a lot that would have to happen for me to move away, but it just feels weird to think about leaving Jubilee."

"Well, I would miss seeing you if I went back to Atlanta."

"If?"

"I mean *when* I go back. I don't foresee any way that I can stay here long term. I hope to just get my mom's finances figured out, help her hire somebody to assist her at the inn, and then go back to my life."

"Do you really think that you can after all of this?"

She shrugged her shoulders. "I don't know. The more I stay here, the more I don't want to leave. But what do I do? I have a career on the rise. I have responsibilities. I have clients. I just don't see how I can leave all of that behind to run this tiny inn. All the dreams I have for myself would be impossible."

"What are those dreams, Heather?"

"I want to get married one day, have kids."

"You don't have to have a big career for that, do you?"

"No, but I want to have a nice home. I want to be able to take vacations and own decent cars. There are a lot of things I want to do, and working at the inn wouldn't provide financially for that."

He chuckled. "You're acting like you'd be alone in that. Wouldn't your husband have a job?"

"I guess you're right. I'm a very independent

woman. I learned it from my mom. I always think in terms of me having to take care of everything."

They stopped for a moment and sat down on a log. "You know whoever you end up choosing as your soulmate, they should be the one taking care of you."

"That's kind of an old timey, chivalrous way of looking at it," she said, smiling.

"I'm just saying a real man will make sure that you're taken care of no matter what. Sure, you can pursue your dreams and work all you want, but you shouldn't have to."

"Well, hopefully, I will find this mystery man one day and he will sweep me off my feet." They continued looking at each other with a long pause in the conversation. Ethan leaned closer, and Heather knew exactly what that meant. He was going to kiss her, and then she was going to be a mess.

"Ethan, I can't. I'm going back to Atlanta soon."

His eyes showed understanding. "I know, but have you ever thought that maybe we were meant to find each other here in Jubilee?"

She smiled slightly before standing up. "We'd better get back to searching."

MADELINE STUMBLED, her foot catching on a root. Brady's strong arms were around her in a millisecond it seemed. He caught her very quickly, and their laughter echoed through the trees. It was a welcome break from the tension of the search. "You need to learn how to navigate these woods," Brady said. "Let me teach you."

She looked at him quizzically. "Do you honestly think I'm the type of person who's ever going to go into the woods alone and get lost?"

"Hey, you never know what might come up, and you need to know this stuff."

She rolled her eyes. "Fine. Go ahead. What do I need to know?" She was actually pretty captivated as Brady explained the basics of forest navigation, the growth of moss, the patterns of the stars, and the call of the birds. Each lesson was a glimpse into his world, the world he'd grown up with that Madeline had missed. His love for the wilderness was evident.

Brady had attached Murphy's leash to his belt so they didn't have to worry about him getting loose. Murphy had kept them on the same path for quite some time, and Brady felt like they were getting close.

They finally stopped for a break, and he spoke about the shopping trip he took with Anna. "She picked out a dress all by herself. It was the cutest thing. She kept twirling in circles, showing it off to me. I think she's really coming out of her shell."

Madeline's heart swelled with pride. "You're an amazing uncle, Brady." She reached down and poured some water into a collapsible cup for Murphy. The dog lapped it up quickly.

Brady's eyes were warm as they met hers, and their lips came together in a sweet lingering kiss. "We make a good team, you and me. In everything."

The search continued until they finally stopped at the end of a path. Murphy barked and pulled sharply to the left where they saw the Lancaster family sitting on a big rock. Their relief and joy was palpable. Dawson immediately stood up and walked over to Brady.

"You have no idea how good it is to see you. I don't even know your name, but I'm really thankful you're here. And you, too, my furry friend," he said, crouching down and kissing Murphy on top of his head.

Brady laughed. "I'm Brady, and this is Madeline. I've been lost out in these woods many times, but y'all don't look worse for the wear. You must have had some food and water to hold you over."

"We don't have any more," Julie said. "We were

out of food, and our water just ran out about an hour ago. We're so thankful you found us."

"There's a whole search party out here looking for you," Madeline said. "I'm going to text them and let them know that we found you."

"Are you ready to head back to the inn?" Brady asked.

They all stood up and walked toward him like moths to a flame. "You have no idea," Dylan said, crossing his arms.

THE DINING ROOM at the inn was filled with the aroma of freshly brewed coffee, sizzling bacon, and fluffy pancakes. Laughter and lively conversation permeated the room as the Lancasters joined Lanelle, Heather, and Ethan at the large family table. It had certainly been an eventful couple of days for the family. Julie's eyes were wide as she recounted the whole ordeal, her voice quivering at times.

"I kept hearing noises in the darkness. Crackling twigs, rustling leaves. I was terrified. I couldn't see anything. I didn't know what in the world might be out there." Dawson's hand reached for hers and squeezed it reassuringly.

"We were all scared, honey, but we stayed together and we got through it just like families do."

Dylan's face, on the other hand, lit up with excitement. "I heard an owl, and I heard something growling. It was like a real adventure like you see in movies. Wait until I tell my friends at school."

Lanelle laughed. "You certainly had an unforgettable experience, young man, and you can tell them a little white lie that you saw Bigfoot out there, too."

They continued to share stories, the terror of the night giving way to the joy of their survival. Lanelle and Heather worked together in the kitchen serving plates filled with delicious food, and the family seemed to eat more than they typically would. After being out in the woods for so long and having little food, they were very hungry.

Heather noticed that Ethan's eyes met hers more times than she could count. They shared knowing glances, and she knew that their relationship had quickly gone beyond friendship. She'd never met a man where she felt such an instant attraction. She'd had many guys in her life over the years that she'd dated for short-term or long-term, but never had she met someone that she instantly connected with like she did with him.

"So what are you planning to do today?" Lanelle

asked Julie.

"Well, I kind of want to stay in the room because I'm a little scared to even walk outside at this point."

Everybody laughed.

"We're actually going to go out and do a little sightseeing today," Dawson interjected, "but we're not getting anywhere near those woods. I think we'll stay on the paved roads for this little outing. We're going to hit some of the shops on the square, maybe do some scenic drives, but don't worry. We'll make sure we have our cell phones, a GPS, and plenty of food and water."

Again, everybody laughed. Heather liked these people and wished that they lived locally. Maybe she would go visit their beach town one day as she really loved the ocean.

After breakfast was over and every plate cleaned up, Ethan pulled her to the side in the living room and handed her a cup of coffee.

"Heather, I want to ask you something."

"Is this a marriage proposal?" she joked.

"You'd feel really bad if it was," he said, smiling.

"What is it?"

He took a deep breath. His nerves very evident.

"Would you go on a date with me to The Buzzed Bear? Have dinner and some drinks?"

Heather's reaction was a mix of surprise and anxiety.

"Ethan, I'm not sure that's a good idea. I'm only here temporarily. We've talked about this."

"I know, but I feel something between us, don't you?"

Heather's heart was pounding at this point. She'd never felt her emotions in such turmoil. She did feel something, something very strong and undeniable, and that was terrifying to her. She was afraid of what it might mean. It was going to make her decision on whether to stay in Jubilee or not even that much harder. It was already difficult enough to think about leaving her mother, but yet she knew she had to do it. She knew she couldn't just give up her entire life so easily.

"Ethan, I'm going back to Atlanta. I have a life there."

"Just one date, Heather. That's all I'm asking."

She looked into his eyes and noticed the sincerity. Hope. Maybe something even a little more than that. She sighed and nodded.

"All right, Ethan. One date."

He smiled broadly. "Thank you. You won't regret it."

She thought to herself that she already was

regretting it. She didn't need to get more attached to this man who was going back to Texas while she went back to Atlanta. It seemed like the silliest thing to do.

Ethan headed out for his day of doing whatever it was he did to study the town. She never quite understood exactly what he was out there doing, and she didn't ask because her cup was already full trying to take care of the inn and her mother. She knew it was time to have a conversation with her mom again. They seemed to get interrupted every time they tried to really talk about things.

She walked back into the kitchen and sat down at the breakfast table.

"Mama, I need to talk to you about something."

"Have you made a decision about staying?" Lanelle asked.

Heather's heart ached at the hope in her mother's eyes.

"Mama, I might stay long enough just to get the finances in order and find more help around here, but I can't promise any more than that."

Lanelle's disappointment was obvious on her face. "I understand, darling. I had just hoped…"

Heather's eyes filled with tears. "I know, Mama. I know."

They sat in silence, the weight of the unspoken words hanging heavy between them.

"I guess I had just always hoped that you would have this longing to come home. I did when I was your age. I couldn't wait to come back and run the inn. I just always assumed you would feel the same way."

She touched her mother's hand. "I know. I do love Jubilee and all the people here, and I do miss home, but I worked really hard to build my business, and walking away from that is really hard for me to think about. It's not just the money that I make, but it's the life that I've built and the friendships."

Even as she said it, Heather knew that wasn't really what it was about. She had friendships in Atlanta, but they were nothing like the ones she had in Jubilee. It was really just the pride of it all. She had built something, and she felt silly giving it all up and coming home, like she was a failure.

"Well, you keep thinking about it and let me know," Lanelle said.

Heather knew that her mother was worried that she would end up having to let go of the inn or sell it to someone else if Heather didn't want to take it over. It was a lot of pressure, even if her mother wasn't saying those words.

CHAPTER 9

The sun was shining brightly overhead, casting a glow over the bright red barn. The smell of hay and leather filled the air as Brady led Bella out of her stall. Anna's eyes were wide with excitement, but he knew she was also a bit nervous as she approached the horse. She had been working up her courage to pet the horses more often. Her little hand reached out and stroked Bella's soft nose.

"Isn't she beautiful?" Brady asked, his voice filled with affection and love for this horse.

"She's so pretty." Anna's voice was filled with wonder.

Brady smiled, encouraging her. "Are you ready to learn how to ride her?" Anna looked shocked but nodded eagerly.

Jasmine appeared in the doorway of the barn smiling. "If my little girl gets hurt, big brother, you're going to have to answer to me."

Brady's laughter rang out across the farm. "Don't you worry, Jasmine. I'm going to take good care of her. I taught you how to ride, after all."

She rolled her eyes. "If I remember it correctly, Grandpa taught me how to ride while you laughed as I fell off the first time." She turned to walk back into the barn. "I'm going to be watching you," she called out behind her.

As Brady began teaching Anna how to ride the horse, his instructions were clear, patient, and filled with many years of experience. First, he started by teaching Anna how to properly groom the horse, showing her how to use a curry comb to loosen the dirt, followed by a body brush to remove it.

"Always brush in the direction of the hair growth," he said, guiding her little hand. Her movements were gentle and tentative at first, but she became more confident as she got familiar with the feel of the horse.

Then he showed her how to put the saddle on Bella, explaining the different parts of an English saddle - the pommel, the cantle, the stirrups. He taught her how to check the girth, making sure it was snug, but not too tight.

"Remember to always approach a horse from the side. Never come up on them from behind." His voice was very firm because he wanted Anna to take safety seriously. She was very focused for an eight-year-old, her little mind absorbing every single word, every single detail.

Once Bella was saddled and ready, Brady helped Anna mount the horse. He showed her how to put her left foot into the stirrup and then swing her right leg over before sitting down on the saddle.

"Keep your back straight, your heels down, and your toes up," he instructed. She adjusted her position. "Now hold the reins with both of your hands, keep your thumbs on top and your fingers closed." Anna's grip was a bit too tight, and her body was tense. "Relax, Anna. Feel the horse beneath you. Move with her."

With Jasmine coming out of the barn to watch closely, Brady led Bella at a walk, Anna's body slowly relaxing. Her movements became more and more fluid. "Let's try a trot. Squeeze your legs, then release. That's how you tell Bella to go faster." Bella broke into a trot and Anna's eyes widened. "Good, Anna. That's it." Brady's voice was filled with pride.

They practiced the trot for several minutes, and Anna's confidence grew. She grinned, her laughter filling the space around them. Brady could tell that Jasmine was so proud of her daughter as she watched her master the basics of riding.

As Brady's instructions continued, teaching Anna how to turn, how to stop, how to communicate with Bella using her body, she got better and better. "Riding is about partnership, communication, and trust," he explained. Anna's skills grew with every moment, and her love for the horse was evident with every touch and glance. When she finally stopped, Brady was so proud of her. "You did great, Anna. For your first time, that was amazing. You're a natural."

Anna's little face glowed as she looked at him. "Can we do this again tomorrow?"

He laughed. "Absolutely." They returned Bella to her stall and the three of them headed back into the house. Brady was so happy to have that feeling of family he had been longing for, for years.

THE DINING ROOM of the inn was a hive of activity as lunch came to a close. After having a good twenty-four hours of rest and being able to actually sightsee without getting lost, the Lancasters were leaving Jubilee today to head back to Seagrove, South Carolina. They had asked that all the search group come over to the inn for a luncheon, so they could thank everyone properly.

Plates clattered and laughter filled the air, the hum of conversation blending into the background. The search group, which consisted of Heather, Ethan, Brady, Madeline, Geneva, and the sheriff, among other deputies, were all gathered around the dining table and in extra chairs that had been brought in. They shared a final meal with the family they'd rescued. Everyone was now filled with smiles and laughter instead of worried faces.

Dawson stood up from his chair and smiled before clearing his throat. The room quieted. "I don't quite know how to thank you all for what you've done for my family. We were lost and scared and you, the people of this community, literally saved us. I don't know how much longer we could have made it out there without food or water, and I've learned that I need to study more about survivalism just in case something like this ever happens again."

Julie spoke up. "Nothing like this is ever happening again because I'm only going to look at trees as I pass them in my car." Everybody laughed.

Dawson looked down at his son. "I'm thankful that we were able to have this experience as a family, even though it was scary and awful, but that I got to show my son how communities can work together. Much like our community back in Seagrove, Jubilee is like a sister city in my mind now because I know the people here are every bit as good as the people in Seagrove. You really banded together to help strangers, and I will be forever grateful for that. You have shown us kindness, compassion and, from the bottom of our hearts, we want to thank you." A round of applause broke out as Dawson sat back down dabbing at his eyes. Heather actually felt a lump in her throat as she was moved by the sincerity of his words.

Julie stood up next and smiled. "We came to Jubilee for a vacation, a little break from our lives by the sea. We wanted to take our son on his very first hike, and, honestly, I can say from the bottom of my heart, it will be the very last hike I ever take." Again people laughed. "We never expected ourselves to be in such a situation, but isn't that how life is? You're just walking along, happily looking around, and then suddenly you find yourself in a predicament, and without the help and love of other people, you can't get out of it. So I just also want to say thank you so much. We never expected to be touched so deeply by the people of Jubilee, and we will never forget you." She looked at each member of the search group, her eyes lingering a bit longer on Geneva, the seasoned guide who knew the forest like the back of her hand and sent everybody in particular directions to make sure that the Lancasters were found.

"Geneva, I learned about your wisdom and knowledge of these woods after the fact, and I just want to say, as a woman, I am so proud that there is somebody like you in Jubilee who can literally guide people out of the darkest place I've ever seen. And I want to thank Brady for actually finding us and leading us out of that forest like it was nothing. I also want to thank Lanelle and Heather for opening up their home to us. This place has been a refuge and was a wonderful place to come back to after our ordeal. You have treated us like family, and we will never forget you. We might come back and visit one day, but I think I'll just stay on the sidewalk rather than going anywhere near that scary, scary forest."

She looked at her son. "Dylan, do you have anything to say to the group?"

Dylan stood up, a big grin on his face. "I'm going to tell everyone at school about the waterfall and the cool noises in the forest, and I am going to tell them that I saw Bigfoot." Everybody started laughing as he sat down and took another yeast roll from the middle of the table.

After lunch, goodbyes were said, bags were packed, and the Lancasters prepared to leave. They hugged as many people as they could and promised to stay in touch before going out and loading up their truck. Heather stood on the porch watching them leave and waved her hand as they disappeared down the road.

"They'll be okay," Ethan said from beside her.

"I don't doubt it. They seem like a wonderful family. I wish they could live here. I'm sure they'll come back, but it might take them a few years to work up the courage."

THE NEXT FEW days were a blur as Madeline started working closer with Jasmine. She was doing great as an assistant. She had all of Madeline's social media postings scheduled out for at least the next thirty days. She had spoken to two bookstores about doing book signings, and she had reserved her a spot on a very popular podcast that featured authors. Madeline was impressed. Jasmine was a go-getter, and she was easing into the role of her assistant like it was nothing.

Today, Madeline was taking a little time off to go visit with Brady at the farm. Her laughter rang through the air as Gilbert, his mischievous goat, nudged her again. Brady stood nearby, smiling as he watched Madeline learn the quirks of farm life.

"I swear this goat has it out for me," Madeline exclaimed, pushing Gilbert away for the hundredth time. Her hands were filled with feed, and she was trying to distribute it equally among the other farm animals, but Gilbert was having none of it.

Brady walked over to help. "Gilbert has just taken a liking to you. He's got a personality, that one."

Together, they went about the routine of feeding the animals. Brady always liked to explain the different personalities and habits of each one. Madeline tried to listen, but he got very in depth about some of them, and she thought he was spending way too much time with the farm animals. This farm life was a far cry from her previous life in the city, but somehow she had embraced it wholeheartedly.

As they worked, their conversation naturally turned to Brady's plans for rebuilding the house. They walked past the construction site where the land had started to be cleared the day before. The temporary trailer they were living in stood nearby, cozy, but a crowded solution.

"I'm making the house bigger this time," Brady said, looking at the blueprints he had rolled out on a bench nearby. "Anna and Jasmine need their own space, and I want to make sure there's plenty of room for all of us."

Madeline looked at the plans. "It's going to be beautiful, Brady, and so thoughtful for you to consider everyone's needs. I still can't believe how much my life has changed since I left the city. I never would've imagined at this time last year that I would be standing out here excited to feed a goat."

He reached out, lifting her chin so their eyes met. "Best change ever?"

She leaned in and kissed him lightly. "Absolutely. Best change ever."

BRADY LOOKED over at his sister as they both hovered around Anna, like two helicopter parents. Anna was running around her room trying to pick out last-minute clothing for her first day at her new school. He could see the excitement in her eyes, probably mixed with a little hint of nervousness.

"You need any help, sweetheart?" Brady asked as he leaned against the doorframe of her bedroom and watched her rummage around in her closet.

"No, Uncle Brady, I can do it." Anna's voice was firm, full of that second-grader independence that she had recently discovered. Riding horses had seemed to give her some newfound confidence.

Jasmine laughed as she sat down on the edge of Anna's bed. "Well, at least let me help you with your hair." Her hair was all over the place, as it typically was. Blonde and curly, it stuck up in multiple directions when she woke up in the morning.

Anna finally decided on her new bright blue dress, which was her favorite color from what she had told Brady. Jasmine started working on braiding her hair. Brady left the room to give them some space and moved into the kitchen to prepare Anna's lunchbox. He had been taking care of her lunch since they moved into the temporary trailer, but now he was packing one for her first day at school. Even though he didn't have kids of his own, it felt like he did right now.

He made a sandwich and cut it up before putting some fruit in a bowl and putting the top on it. "Uncle Brady," Anna's voice rang out from across the trailer, "can I have those cheese crackers you bought yesterday?"

"Sure thing, Anna Banana," he called back.

As he packed her lunch, he thought about how far they had come in the few weeks that she had been there. She had been through so much, but she was quite resilient for a little eight-year-old girl.

Once they got everything ready, they ran out the door, all three of them, and jumped into his truck, driving down the winding road to Jubilee Elementary School. Anna was talking nonstop about who she thought her new teacher would be, what she would be like, whether she'd make new friends, and what subjects she might learn about in school.

Jasmine kept the conversation going, asking her what she wanted to be when she grew up. Brady listened, smiling as Anna said that she wanted to become a veterinarian and work with horses.

"Maybe we can go visit the vet clinic one day," Jasmine said. "You can see what they do there." Anna's eyes widened with excitement. Brady made a mental note to talk to one of his friends that worked at a veterinary clinic and ask if he could bring Anna by.

As they went over the hill, the school came into view and Anna's chatter suddenly stopped. It got very quiet in the truck suddenly. "It's going to be fine, sweetie," Jasmine reassured her.

"I know," Anna said, but her voice was quivering a little.

They pulled into the parking lot, and Brady turned off the engine. Together, they walked Anna to her class, her little hand tightly gripping Brady's. They had become very close since Jasmine came back to Jubilee, and Brady was so happy about it. He loved having that feeling of family around him, and Anna brought a certain energy to his life that hadn't been there before.

"And you remember what I told you, right?" Brady whispered to her as he leaned down when they reached the door of her classroom.

"That I can call you anytime if I need you."

"That's right. You just go to the office and tell them you need to call your uncle Brady. I know everybody here, and they'll let you call me."

With a deep breath, she nodded, squared up her shoulders, and walked into her new classroom. Brady and Jasmine stood there for a moment, like they didn't know what to do. They watched her through the classroom window. Brady felt a little lump in his throat as he watched his niece take her seat looking so tiny, yet so brave.

"She's going to be fine," Jasmine whispered, squeezing his arm. It might've been just as much for her as him when she said it.

"I know. I just wish I could protect her from everything."

The ride home was quieter without Anna. Brady could feel Jasmine's eyes on him, studying him. "You really love her, don't you?" she asked.

"With all my heart," Brady replied, not taking his eyes off the road.

"I was a little worried about it when we came back to town. I didn't know how you would react to me having a kid that you didn't know about."

"Well, it was a surprise for sure."

"I know you don't approve of her father, of course, after all the things he's done."

"No, I do not approve. And, honestly, if I saw him in real life, I can't promise what I would do."

"You're a good man, Brady. When we were kids, I always wondered if you'd grow up to be like Grandpa or Dad, but I think you might even be better."

"I don't know if that's possible, but I always try."

"Well, I want to thank you for everything you've done for me and Anna."

“You're my family, both of you. I would do anything for y'all."

They rode in silence for a minute before she spoke up again. "And I know you love Madeline. I've never seen you act that way about any woman."

"I do love Madeline. She's the best thing to happen to me in my life."

"Well, don't ruin it," Jasmine said, laughing as she punched him in the arm lightly.

"Don't worry, I don't plan to."

CHAPTER 10

Heather stared at her reflection in the mirror. It had been a long time since she'd been out on a date. Longer than she cared to admit. Back in Atlanta, she was always busy working, and that was basically her social life, aside from eating big tubs of ice cream while she took a nice hot bath after a long day.

"You look beautiful," Lanelle said from the doorway.

"Thanks, Mama," Heather said, forcing a smile. "I hope so."

"You'll have a great time. Just be yourself as always. And Ethan's a wonderful guy."

Heather nodded. "He is a nice guy. I really enjoy spending time with him."

She heard a polite knock on the door and turned to see Ethan standing in the doorway, looking handsome as ever, wearing a collared shirt and a pair of slacks. She hadn't seen him dressed up like that yet, but he looked good.

"Ready to go?" he asked.

"I'm ready," Heather said, grabbing her purse and heading out the door. They waved goodbye to Lanelle as they walked up the sidewalk toward The Buzzed Bear. It wasn't that far from the inn, and it was a beautiful evening to take a walk.

As usual, they chatted easily as they walked along, conversation flowing effortlessly. Heather asked questions about Ethan's research into Jubilee and other small towns, and he always had some nugget of information to share. When they got to The Buzzed Bear, they sat in a booth across from the bar and ordered a couple of drinks. Ethan got a glass of wine while Heather got a margarita, which wasn't something she did often.

As usual, the ambiance of The Buzzed Bear was cozy, with a mix of rustic charm and modern elegance. Heather and Ethan sat at the booth chatting while patrons around them had conversations that gave a great background noise.

"So, Heather, you've told me a lot about the inn

and Jubilee, but I want to know more about you. What makes Heather tick? What do you like to do when you're not here helping your mom or back in Atlanta, taking care of everybody's finances?"

She smiled. "I don't do a whole lot. I'm not exactly a person who has hobbies. Honestly, when I'm back in Atlanta, I work a lot. I can't even have a pet because I don't have time for it."

"So then coming to Jubilee must be a nice break for you right now."

"You would think so, but I'm constantly getting emails and being bombarded with calls from my boss. He didn't want me to take this time off, so I feel really pushed to go back sooner rather than later."

"Why would you want a job like that?" Ethan asked. "I mean, maybe I'm spoiled because I get to keep my own hours and do what I want to do, but it just seems like that's a lot of stress."

She smiled slightly. "I love numbers. I'm a geek that way, I guess. And I like what I do, but sometimes it is a little much. It takes over my life. I think it's one of the reasons I haven't gotten married or started a family because I was just so busy chasing that career. Now it feels like time is ticking away, and maybe I'm making a mistake going back there."

She couldn't tell for sure, but she thought his

eyebrows raised a bit like there was hope that she might stay in Jubilee, and maybe there was. She felt conflicted about it. Moment to moment, she made a different decision in her mind.

"But you don't think being in Jubilee is going to let you have a successful career?"

"No, I don't see how. I would have to take over the inn, and that would be a lot of work. And I just don't see how I could continue in the finance industry if I lived here. It's not like there are a lot of big businesses here that would allow me to have clients."

"But everything's pretty much virtual nowadays, isn't it?"

"Yeah, I suppose so. I mean, I've been able to do some work while I've been here, although it has been hard because I've been distracted by my mother and people lost in the forest."

He laughed. "Yeah, that was a little bit distracting. So if you could have a hobby, what would you like to do?"

She thought for a moment.

"You're going to laugh at me."

"No, I won't. I promise."

"Well, when I was in college, I really enjoyed painting."

"Painting? Really?"

"Yeah, landscapes mostly because of what I'm surrounded by here. The mountains and even the woods would inspire me. So, I think if I had a hobby, I would paint."

He smiled. "I can imagine that. I can see you back here in Jubilee sitting on the front porch of All Tucked Inn, looking at the mountains and painting them. I can see it in my mind."

"I'm glad you can. I have a hard time picturing the future. I feel like I'm going to make one wrong mistake, and everything's going to go off the rails."

"I'm sure you already know this, but making a mistake doesn't mean that it can't be undone," Ethan said, chuckling.

"I know. I guess I'm kind of a perfectionist. I really don't like to make mistakes."

"It's hard to go through life being perfect."

"Yes, and it's exhausting. I think that's why I'm going through such a struggle about this. I really don't know what to do. I'm afraid I'm going to make the wrong decision, and I'm either going to leave my mother in the lurch or I'm going to find myself hating my life one way or the other."

"I think the best thing to do is just take it one step at a time. My grandmother used to say that you just need to make the next right decision, whatever that is, and I've tried to live my life that way. I think when you look out way ahead of you, it can be super overwhelming."

She knew he was right. It was good advice, and she wished that she had met his grandmother. She sounded like a wise woman.

They spent the next hour ordering food and chatting over drinks. Heather loved how comfortable she felt around Ethan. It wasn't an effort to make small talk with him. They just clicked. They laughed, cut up, and told stories. She learned a lot more about his high school years and how much of a geek he thought he was. He told her he wasn't in the popular crowd because he was so into history and nobody else was.

She talked about being in high school in Jubilee and how boring it was. There wasn't a whole lot to do in such a small town for a high school kid. She dreamed of going to the big city and then as soon as she could, she left and went to Atlanta to start her career after college.

They had dessert, which was strawberry shortcake, and then it was time to go.

"Listen, I don't want our date to be over yet, so I

was wondering if you might want to do something else with me?" Ethan asked.

"What would that be?" Heather wracked her brain because Jubilee still wasn't a hotbed of activity, especially at night. Some people said the sidewalks rolled up at five o'clock, and that was pretty much true. Most of the places in town were closed no later than six o'clock except for the tavern and a couple of small restaurants. Other than that, everybody was home, comfortable, probably in their pajamas by seven o'clock every night.

"I was thinking maybe we could go play mini golf."

Heather hadn't thought anything about mini golf in many years. She used to go there in high school with her friends. They would go on Friday nights, play mini golf and then get ice cream. It brought back wonderful memories, and she had forgotten the place was even still open.

"You know what? I would love to do that, but I just want to warn you that I have a lot of experience at mini golf, and I'm probably going to beat you really badly."

He started laughing. "How do you know I'm not really experienced at mini golf?"

"Well, after you telling me about your childhood

and growing up on the farm, I think cow tipping was something you were familiar with. But I bet mini golf was not something you did a lot of."

Ethan laughed, "I guess we'll see who is the master of mini golf then." The bill came to the table and Ethan reached for it, pulling his wallet out of his back pocket.

"Let me help you with that. I can pay my half."

He stared at her like she was insane. "You've been living in the city too long."

“What is that supposed to mean?”

“When a man asks a woman out on a date, he pays for it. Otherwise, he doesn’t need to be taking women out on dates." He reached in his wallet and got his credit card out, handing it to the server.

"You know it's the twenty-first century," she said, playfully.

"I know that, but women aren't supposed to pay for dates. That's the man's job."

"I think that might be a little bit of an ancient way of thinking, but I appreciate it nonetheless." Inside, her stomach was full of butterflies. She had been raised with chivalrous men, and she actually did expect a man to pay for the date. But ever since moving to the city, she found that that wasn't the same way everywhere. She had been on several dates where the man picked up the check, put down cash for his half of it, and then stared at her. She had become accustomed to that, and it wasn't a good thing.

"Let me tell you something, Heather. If you're dating men, whether it's in the city or up here in the mountains, that don't think you're worth paying for on a date, then you don't need to be dating those men." He was very serious as he looked at her, and it made her stomach flip and flop. Thankfully, the server came back quickly and handed him the check to sign.

Heather had to admit that chivalry was something she did miss when she wasn't in Jubilee. It seemed to be a dying art in the suburbs and the cities, so she was very glad to see it was alive and well in a man like Ethan.

"Ready to go?" he asked.

"Absolutely. I'm ready to mop the floor with you on the mini golf course," she said laughing.

They walked out into the cool night air. It wasn't fall quite yet, and it was still very hot during the day, but the evenings were starting to get cooler and cooler.

"I love seeing the courthouse lit up at night,"

Ethan said as they walked down the sidewalk toward the square.

The courthouse, which was made of red brick with white trim, stood like a castle in the middle of the square. Lights lit it up from below, and it was a beautiful sight to behold on a dark night.

"Are you sure you're okay walking all the way to the mini golf place?"

"Yeah, it's not that far," Heather said, wishing that she had worn better shoes.

They continued walking and chatting until they went around the corner to the other side street where the mini golf place was. Ethan paid, of course, and then they each got their golf clubs and a ball and went out onto the course.

This place brought back so many memories for Heather. It was often the place that they went to have fun on a Friday or Saturday night, that is if they weren't at the skating rink or the movie theater, and occasionally the bowling alley. Those were the only four places to go in Jubilee when she was a teenager, and not much had changed. They added the tavern, which gave the older people a place to go. But other than that, the town was stuck in time, and that was not a bad thing.

The neon glow of the mini golf course looked

like an almost surreal landscape. Heather and Ethan took their clubs and headed to the first hole. It was a whimsical course filled with all kinds of interesting features like castles and windmills. They were old, and many of them were exactly the same as Heather remembered them, repainted over the years, but still standing strong.

"You know," Ethan said, swinging his golf club and missing the ball completely. "I might have exaggerated my mini golf prowess just a bit."

Heather burst into laughter. "Oh, really? Well, maybe I'll go easy on you then," she teased.

She effortlessly guided her ball toward the hole. As the game progressed, each of them taking their turns and sometimes succeeding and sometimes failing spectacularly, their laughter rang through the night. They teased each other, made silly bets, and occasionally offered a genuine compliment on a particularly good shot.

Ethan was quite the gentleman as usual, allowing Heather to win the first few holes and pretending he couldn't play the game. But then she realized he was holding back.

"Come on, Ethan. You have to show me what you've got," she challenged.

He smiled and accepted the challenge, and soon

they found themselves engaged in a very spirited battle, each one of them trying to outdo the other one. It was all in good fun, of course, but the connection between them deepened as they shared a playful experience together.

At the end, they reached a particularly challenging hole that had a tricky bridge and a windy path. Ethan's ball ended up stuck under the bridge. He crouched down to retrieve it, and Heather leaned over trying to help. When their heads collided with a gentle thud, they both froze inches apart, their eyes locking. Time seemed to stand still as they looked at each other.

Nobody else was around, and they had the mini golf course all to themselves. Suddenly, Heather realized Ethan's eyes were darkening in intensity, and she felt a magnetic pull drawing her toward him. Slowly, their lips met in a soft, tentative kiss. It was a simple kiss, but it held the promise of something much more profound, something much more real. When they broke apart, each with a smile on their face, there was an understanding passing between them. They tried to continue the game, but it was very apparent that both of them were distracted. Heather wanted to go back to the kissing part, but she knew that probably wasn't the best idea.

When they finished the last hole, Ethan looked at Heather.

"I have never had so much fun losing at mini golf."

"Who said you lost? I think we both won tonight."

HEATHER AND ETHAN walked toward the inn as the night drew to a close. She had had so much fun going out to dinner and playing mini golf with him, and she really didn't want the night to end, but when they looked up ahead and saw the flashing lights of an ambulance in front of the inn, her heart sank. Her mother was there alone with no guests, so she knew exactly what was going on. They both took off running straight toward the inn and walked inside to see Lanelle on a stretcher in the middle of the foyer. She was awake and alert, thankfully, so Heather was able to breathe a sigh of relief.

"Mama, what happened?"

"Oh, silly me. I was trying to get something out of the top cabinet, and I slipped and fell."

"Did you hit your head?" Heather asked, walking over and touching her mother's head.

"No, I don't think so. My neck is kind of hurting, and I hurt my arm when I fell on it."

"How did you get help?"

"Thankfully, my cell phone was in my pocket. You know, old habits die hard. I used to always sit by the phone when you were out late at night, and I was just keeping my phone with me in case you called and needed me."

"I was just around the block, Mama. I wouldn't have needed any help, but I'm glad you had your phone with you."

"Is there anything I can do?" Ethan asked.

"No. Just keep my girl company while I go get looked at."

"Mama, you're not going to the hospital alone. I'm going over there, and I'm sitting with you and bringing you home."

"It's fine, Heather, just stay here."

"No, I'm going there."

"And I'm going with you," Ethan said, looking at Heather.

Lanelle cut her eyes between the two like she wanted to know what little secret they were keeping. "I'm sure I'm fine. I probably just sprained something."

“Well, it's better to be safe than sorry, ma'am," one of the EMTs said. "We need to get her moving."

"Okay. I'll meet you over there in a few minutes. I'll be there as soon as they put you in a room."

"I'll see you there. Don't worry. I'll be okay." Lanelle was just like many mothers, always trying to make sure that her kids weren't worried about her, never wanting to be a burden.

"Oh, my gosh. That scared me to death when I saw that ambulance," Heather said. Ethan pulled her into a tight hug and she had to admit it felt good. It felt good to have someone strong and steady with her. She had barely known this guy for even a couple of weeks, and it felt like she'd known him forever. She felt comfortable with him being there with her in that moment.

"She's going to be okay. Let's grab some water and snacks to put in your bag so that you don't get low blood sugar or something, and we'll head over there."

"Why would I get low blood sugar? We just ate not too long ago," Heather said, laughing.

Ethan shrugged his shoulders. "I don't know. It just seemed like the thing to say in the moment. Let's go."

CHAPTER 11

Heather paced back and forth in the waiting room of the hospital. Ethan sat in the chair, trying to get her to sit down beside him, but she just wasn't having it.

"I don't understand why they won't let me back there."

"Well, because they're probably trying to get her stabilized and figure out exactly what happened."

"You think she's going to be okay, don't you?"

Ethan stood up and put his hands on her shoulders. "Of course, I do. She was talking when they took her. She didn't look like she was in any distress. I'm sure they're just doing all the regular testing. You know the emergency room takes forever."

"I guess so. I just feel so guilty."

"Guilty, why? Because we went out on a date?"

"No, I feel guilty because I haven't been here for years. I haven't come home to take care of my mom or help her with the inn. I'm all she has. She's told me that."

"Heather, you can't be expected to live your life in Jubilee if that's not where you want to be. Your mom understands that, and she has plenty of friends around her."

"Yeah, but friends aren't always the same as family," she said, sitting down.

She leaned over and put her head between her knees. "I hate this!"

"It's all going to be okay. I'm sure of it."

"I'm not very good at waiting," she said, sitting up. "I'm not a very patient person. You should know that about me. I tend to fly off the handle and freak out when things happen."

Ethan chuckled. "I understand, and I'm willing to take the risk."

"You know what happened tonight can't happen again, right?" she said, looking at him with a serious look on her face.

"Why do you say that?"

"Because," before she could finish what she was saying, her phone buzzed. She looked down and saw the name Nathan on the screen. Her boss. Again. He had been calling every day, multiple times a day. "I'm sorry, Ethan. I need to take this. Can you wave to me if they come out?"

"Of course. I'll be right here."

Heather walked out of the sliding glass doors onto the sidewalk and answered the call, her voice tight with frustration. "Nathan, this really isn't a good time."

"I don't care, Heather," he snapped. "The Jennings file is falling apart, and you know that you're the only one who can fix it. We cannot keep letting you stay in Jubilee. This was supposed to be a short visit, and it has become way too extended."

"My mother is in the hospital, Nathan. She fell. I can't just leave her."

"Heather, I'm not a heartless man. But the world does not stop turning because of your personal issues. We're a business and our clients come first, no matter what. I just don't understand what's going on with you. You have always known that the clients come before anything else."

She clenched her fist beside her waist, anger and fear swirling within her. "What about family, Nathan? Don't they come first, too?"

"To be honest? No. You chose this career,

Heather. You knew the sacrifices you'd have to make. And I need you back here now."

Her voice broke, tears threatening to spill over. "I need more time, Nathan. Please."

He sighed, his voice slightly softer, but still unyielding. "I'll give you till the end of the week. That's it. And I expect you back here with that Jennings file sorted out. I need you to call them immediately." The line went dead before Heather could say anything else. Her legs felt weak. She leaned against the wall.

She had spent so many years working her way up to her position in the company, and now things seemed to be tenuous at best. Ethan walked outside, obviously seeing her through the windows. "Hey, what happened? Are you okay?"

She shook her head, tears spilling down her cheeks. "My boss is pressuring me to get back. Our biggest client, work, everything, my mom." At this point, Heather was just babbling. "I just can't leave her. What am I going to do?"

"We'll figure this out," Ethan said. His voice was strong and reassuring. "Let's just focus on your mom right now. We'll deal with your boss later."

They settled back into the waiting area, the

minutes turning into over an hour. Finally, a doctor appeared. His face calm and composed.

"You're Heather? I'm Dr. Harris. I just want you to know your mom's doing well. She didn't actually fall per se. It appears she had a low blood pressure incident, and that caused her to faint."

Heather's eyes widened, "But she told me she fell down."

Dr. Harris shook his head, "She may have said that not to worry you. It's not uncommon in such situations. She has some minor bruising, but nothing serious."

"What would cause her to faint?"

"Oftentimes, it's just dehydration, so we're giving her some fluids. She'll need to rest for a couple of days just to make sure. This is a very common problem, but it is something that she may need help to overcome."

"What do you mean?"

"I mean, I think your mom can't run the inn by herself anymore. She's going to need help, or she's going to have to give it up. With the atrial fibrillation and now passing out, I can tell that she's under stress, and she's not taking care of herself. When she told me how little water she's been drinking, I was astonished she hadn't passed out already."

"Can I see her?"

"Of course. Follow me."

Ethan sat back down, "I'll wait for you here."

Heather followed the doctor down the hallway. Lanelle's room was filled with a soft light. She looked up as her daughter entered and smiled.

"Heather, honey, I didn't want you to worry. I'm fine, really."

Heather leaned down and hugged her mother. "I was so scared, Mama."

"I know. I'm sorry."

"It's not your fault. I just don't understand why you didn't tell me you were struggling so badly. I would've come home weeks or months or years ago."

"Because like I told you before, I just wanted you to come home on your own. I didn't want to make you come home."

MADELINE STRETCHED her arms above her head, a smile crossing her face. She'd been working tirelessly on her book for the last few hours, and her fingers were starting to go numb. She looked over at Jasmine, who was still busily working on social media graphics. Jasmine had done so well at this job that she now didn't know what she would do without her. She had quickly become her right hand. She was by far more helpful than Madeline's ex-husband and ex-best friend had been.

"You're doing a great job with those graphics, Jasmine," Madeline said as she stood up and walked over behind her. "They look so professional and eye-catching. I couldn't have ever done that myself."

Jasmine looked up at her. "Thanks so much, Madeline. Your encouragement always means the world to me."

"Well, it's the truth. Now, how about I whip up some lunch for us? Sandwiches sound good?"

"That sounds great. I'm starving."

"Okay, you keep working and I'll go take care of the food."

"Thank you," Jasmine said as Madeline left the room and shut the door behind her.

"I'll be right back," Madeline called behind her as she headed towards the kitchen.

When she got to the kitchen and opened the refrigerator, a thought occurred to her. She wasn't sure what kind of cheese Jasmine liked on her sandwich. "Hey, Jasmine, do you want American cheese or Swiss cheese on your sandwich?" She called loudly. No response.

She didn't want to have to walk all the way back over to the office, but she figured that was her only option. She walked back toward the door, her footsteps soft on the wooden floor since she was wearing socks. When she got to the door, she could hear Jasmine's voice. It was low and tense speaking on the phone.

"Please, just stop. I know. No, I can't. You have to understand, I have a life here now. I'm starting over. You can't ask that of me. I'll try to visit, but please don't be angry." Madeline's heart just stopped, a chill running down her spine. She knew exactly who Jasmine was talking to. Her abusive ex-husband who was incarcerated. The man who had nearly destroyed her life and Anna's. Why on earth was she talking to him? Why was she putting herself back in that position when her life was just starting to get back on track?

Without thinking, Madeline pushed the door open, her eyes wide with shock, and Jasmine looked up at her. Her face was pale. Her eyes filled with worry. "Madeline... I didn't hear you." The phone went silent and Jasmine ended the call, her hands shaking as she set it back on the desk.

"What was that about?" Madeline demanded. She was upset on behalf of Anna and Brady and herself for giving Jasmine a chance. "Was that him? That was your ex-husband."

Jasmine's face crumbled, and tears spilled over her cheeks. "Yes. Yes, it was. Please, Madeline, don't tell Brady. He'll go to jail looking for him when he gets out. He'll do something crazy."

Madeline's mind was reeling as emotions turned into a whirlwind of betrayal, confusion, and fear. "Why, Jasmine? Why would you talk to him after everything he's done to you?"

Jasmine continued to sob. "He called me. He said he was sorry, that he's changed, that he's been going to church while he's in jail. I know it's all a lie, but I felt sorry for him. I felt like I had to be nice. You gave me a second chance. Maybe he deserves one, too."

"You felt sorry for him?" Madeline's voice was incredulous. "He hurt you, Jasmine. He hurt you in front of your daughter. He broke you, and you feel sorry for him?"

"I know it's stupid. I know. I don't know what came over me. This is just part of the abuse cycle, I guess. I'm so scared that I'm going to end up back with him. I don't want to go back to that life, but I know he's never going to leave me alone."

Madeline's anger dissolved, replaced by a deep

compassion. She sat down in her chair and rolled closer to Jasmine. "It's okay, Jasmine. We will figure this out. You have to talk to your therapist about this. You have to learn to work through this cycle of going back to him. It's simply not an option. Don't you like working for me?"

"Of course I do. It's the best thing that's happened to me since my daughter was born."

"Well, you can't work for me if you're going to go back with him. I don't want any involvement with a man like that."

"I understand. And he's in jail for a while yet."

"Yes, Jasmine, but you talking to him on the phone or going to visit him is out of the question. Can we agree on that?"

"Yes, I agree. But you can't tell Brady. I don't want him getting in trouble for me."

"I understand. I don't like it, but I won't tell Brady. But you have to promise me that you won't talk to that man again. You have to cut him off completely. In fact, go change your phone number today."

"Change my phone number? But I have his daughter."

"He gave up his right to be her father when he abused you for years right in front of her. You also need to go get a restraining order or something if you don't already have it, because when he gets out and comes looking for you, you need to be protected legally."

"I know you're right. I'm just not thinking clearly."

"Are you still going to your therapy sessions?"

"I've missed the last couple. I thought I was doing better. I love this job, and I felt like I was getting back to my normal self."

"Well, I think we can both see that you still need to be going, and you need to be honest with your therapist about this."

“I know, you're right. I will. I'll make an appointment right now."

"I know you can do this, Jasmine. You're a strong woman. You just don't see it yet."

Madeline walked back out of the room to go make the sandwiches still not knowing what kind of cheese Jasmine liked, but it felt like a silly question to ask in the moment. As she stood in the kitchen staring into the refrigerator mindlessly, she felt extreme guilt for not telling Brady what happened. But Jasmine was right. If Brady knew that she was talking to her ex-husband on the phone from prison, he would definitely have a problem with that. It might ruin his relationship with his sister that he was working so hard to build. But worse yet, he might go to that jail and do something that would put him on the other side of the bars.

HEATHER'S HANDS had not stopped moving all morning. As she folded the freshly washed linens to get ready for the next set of guests, her mind was racing with all the tasks that awaited her. In the midst of that, she was also thinking about her clients and the next phone call she would inevitably receive from Nathan.

She could hear her mother humming in the living room, a comforting melody, but another reminder that she was doing something she wasn't supposed to be doing since coming home from the hospital.

"Mama, you're supposed to be resting," Heather called out as she walked into the living room and saw that her mother was rearranging something on the mantle. "You just got home from the hospital. Let me handle things."

"Heather, I'm not an invalid," Lanelle's voice

snapped, laced with frustration. "I can help. I don't want to sit around here feeling useless."

It was a conundrum that Heather had not been able to figure out. Her mother wanted her to come home and help with the inn, but she didn't want her to do everything. She wanted to still feel like she was vital and useful in the business.

Heather sighed. She knew this argument well. Her mother had pride and a sense of independence that were unmatched.

"I know, Mama. I just worry about you. Let me take care of things, at least for today."

Lanelle's reply was stubborn silence as she sank back down into the recliner by the window. Heather had set her up with snacks and drinks and her favorite TV shows, but Lanelle hated all of it. For now, though, Heather knew she had won the argument.

Once the linens were neatly folded, Heather moved on to prepping food for the next guests. Her hands worked automatically like she'd been doing this for years. She chopped and mixed and found herself thinking about Ethan. Where was he? He'd been gone again all day, and she couldn't shake the nagging curiosity about what he was up to. His presence at the inn had become a comforting constant, and his absence was always felt, especially since their kiss. Even though she had told him that it couldn't happen again, she secretly wanted it to. She knew that wasn't the best thing for either one of them. Ethan would be going home to Texas any day now, and she would be going back to Atlanta. Maybe. She didn't know.

Just as she was thinking, her phone rang, jolting her out of her happy moment. She glanced down at the caller ID and felt a pang of irritation. Nathan, again.

"What now?" she muttered to herself as she answered the call. "Hello, Nathan. How can I help you?"

"Heather, the Jennings file is falling apart. I need you back here. Your clients need you."

Heather's irritation turned into anger. "Nathan, my mother just got out of the hospital, and I'm not leaving her. I've told you this."

"She'll be fine," Nathan insisted, his tone dismissive. "Get back to Atlanta. We need you."

Heather's heart pounded. Anger and resentment in levels she had never felt before bubbled up within her. "Well, maybe I don't need you," she said quietly. There was a long pause.

"Excuse me?" Nathan's voice was incredulous.

"I think you heard me," Heather said, her voice firm. "You know what I'm realizing, Nathan? I'm happy here. I am tired of the pressure, the clients, and your endless demands."

"You can't be serious. You're going to walk away from your career to live in some podunk town in the mountains?"

Heather was glad she was on the phone and not in person because she was pretty sure she would strangle him right now. "This podunk town is the place I grew up. It's the place where my mom is, all of my friends are. It's the place that holds all of my memories. So don't you talk about it like that. Just because you don't have a place that you love or people that love you doesn't mean that I don't."

Nathan let out a growl. "You can't just walk away from all of your clients like this. You're going to ruin your entire reputation."

"You know what? I don't care."

Nathan sighed. "I think you're just being an overly emotional woman right now." Yep, if she had been in person, there would've been strangulation involved.

"Any time a strong woman stands up for herself, we're called emotional. And you know what? We are emotional, because being emotional is not a weakness, Nathan. Maybe if you had ever learned that you would have a happier life that didn't involve you staying at the office twenty hours a day and living off of caffeine."

"Look, you can judge me however you want," he said, irritation evident in his voice, "but this is your last chance. If you don't agree right now that you're coming home tomorrow and getting back to work, then you're fired."

A smile spread across Heather's face. When he said she was fired, there was a relief flowing through her body that she hadn't anticipated. This whole time, she had been going back and forth trying to figure out what to do, feeling conflicted on whether she wanted her life in Atlanta or her life in Jubilee. Something had shifted without her even realizing it.

"You know what? You don't have to fire me, Nathan, because I quit." She pressed end on the call, laid her cell phone on the countertop and smiled. The decision had been made. She was staying in Jubilee. She didn't know what her future held, but for now all she could do was feel relief.

CHAPTER 12

The rest of the afternoon was a whirlwind of activity. Heather didn't let her mother know what had happened on the phone. She didn't want to reveal that until she felt the time was right. Instead, she flitted from task to task, ordering groceries, talking to wedding planners about renting out the space, reorganizing the outdoor space for upcoming weddings, all while ensuring that Lanelle was resting.

Despite her best efforts, Lanelle continued to try to push herself. "I can't just sit here, Heather," she insisted, "I need to do something." Heather's heart was torn between the desire to care for her mother and understanding her need for independence.

"I know, Mama," she said softly, "but your health

has to come first. You took care of me my whole life, so for right now, let me take care of you. I promise you're going to get to feeling better soon."

Her mother didn't know that the reason she would feel better is because Heather was staying and was going to take off a lot of the load. She didn't want to tell her that yet. For some reason, it just didn't feel like the right time. She waited for Ethan to show back up, wondering if he would be back for dinner. For one small moment, she wondered, "Did he just go back home to Texas? Did he check out while she wasn't paying attention? Did he not want to say goodbye?"

Feeling anxious about it, she decided to go up to his room and make sure his bags were still there. Just so she didn't feel bad about herself, she decided she would also change out his towels and linens as they needed to be washed anyway. She walked up the creaky stairs toward his room and tapped on the door just in case she was mistaken, and he had been in there all along. No answer. She slowly opened the door to reveal his bed all made, but his bags were still sitting in the corner, and he still had some shirts hanging up in the closet. Taking a thankful sigh of relief, she sat down on the edge of the bed.

His room was neatly organized just like he was.

Ethan seemed to take meticulous care of himself. Nothing seemed out of place at first glance, but her eyes wandered to the side table next to the bed. She noticed a file lying open. Her heart leapt in her throat as she read the label: *Jubilee's finances*. Her mind spun with confusion and disbelief. What was Ethan doing with this information? Was he even a historian and a writer, or had he been just pretending all along?

Driven by a compulsion that she just couldn't resist, Heather walked over and opened the file, her hands trembling. She didn't want this to be something bad. She had feelings for him, and now she felt like she could throw up. Inside the file, she found an array of documents that made her breath catch in her throat. Maps of Jubilee with certain areas marked, detailed financial records of local businesses, confidential town council meeting notes, and personal information about key residents, including herself and her mother.

A chill ran down her spine as the pieces started to fall into place. He had been gathering information, spying on the town of Jubilee, all under the guise of researching small towns. But why? What was he really after? She felt a level of anger and betrayal bubbling up within her, a burning rage that made her hands shake. How could she have been so blind? How could she have trusted this perfect stranger? It was clear that he had been sent here with a purpose, some hidden agenda that went far beyond his claim of being a historian and a writer.

How had she let this man into her life, her home, and her heart? Had he been lying to her the entire time, using her and manipulating her? She felt betrayed. The wound cut deep beneath the anger and hurt. She still had a glimmer of doubt. Was there more to this story? Was there a reason or a justification for Ethan's actions? She closed the file with her mind racing. She knew she needed to confront Ethan to hear the truth from him. She needed to know why he had done this, why he had deceived her and her mother, but first she was going to let it play out just a bit longer. She would pretend that she hadn't seen anything until the time was right. She wanted to investigate Ethan, while Ethan was investigating her and her town.

IF THERE WAS one good thing about small towns, it was that you could just show up at somebody's house unannounced when you had a problem, and that was exactly what Heather was doing today. She felt terrible just showing up at Geneva's door, but she was the best person she knew to talk to when she needed some wise counsel.

Her heart was a whirlpool of emotions when she parked her car in Geneva's driveway and walked up to the door. She needed somebody to talk to, somebody compassionate who had known her her entire life. Geneva was more than a friend; she was like a surrogate grandmother, or mother, or aunt. It didn't matter.

She knocked on the door. Geneva answered, her wild hair sticking up as she wore an apron with her hands covered in flour. She smiled. Heather could smell the fresh aroma of coffee and something home-cooked coming from inside the cabin.

"Well, isn't this a nice surprise?" she said, smiling. "I would give you a hug, but I would get flour all over you. Come on in. You look like you've seen a ghost."

"I feel like it," Heather admitted as she walked past her and sat down at the breakfast bar on one of the bar stools.

She was still trying to compose herself after quitting her job and then finding out Ethan had been lying the whole time. Geneva's keen eyes didn't miss a thing.

"Okay, something's wrong. What happened?" She leaned against the counter and looked at Heather. Heather sighed, looking down at her hands.

"I've made a decision, Geneva. I'm staying in Jubilee." Geneva's face broke out into a big smile.

"Oh, sweetie, that's wonderful news. I knew you would find your way back home. I'm sure your mother is tickled pink about it."

"I haven't told her yet."

"Why on earth haven't you told her?"

"I don't know. I was just waiting for the right moment. A lot has happened today."

"Well, it's good news. Certainly your mother will be glad to hear it."

"It's not that simple, there's something else, something about Ethan." Geneva's smile faded, replaced by a look of concern.

"What about him?"

"I found something in his room," she started, her voice breaking. "Files, information about Jubilee and its finances, other things that made me realize he's not just here for a book. He's been spying on all of us, Geneva." Her eyes widened as she reached across the counter to take Heather's hand.

"Hold on now. Let's not jump to conclusions. Tell me everything." Heather poured out the story explaining in detail everything she'd found in Ethan's room. She talked about her own anger and betrayal. The words just fell out of her mouth, each one a painful reminder of the trust she'd placed in Ethan. She felt silly for being so blind. Someone else who wasn't wanting the romance of it all probably would've seen this coming from a mile away. Geneva listened, her eyes soft and understanding.

When Heather was finally done retelling the story, she took in a deep breath and said, "Heather, I know you're angry and you have every right to be, but are you sure you know the whole truth?"

"The whole truth?" Heather's voice rose. "What else is there to know? He lied to me, Geneva. He lied to all of us."

Geneva's hand squeezed Heather's. "I know, dear, but people do things for all the strangest reasons. Sometimes good people make mistakes. Sometimes they have reasons that aren't immediately clear."

"He's been deceitful, Geneva. I can't just overlook that. How could I ever trust him again?"

"Trust is a fragile thing, Heather, but it can be rebuilt. You and Ethan have something special. Don't throw that away without hearing his side of the story. Look at Brady and Jasmine, they're rebuilding their relationship as siblings after the trust had been broken."

She sat there silently. "I don't know if I can."

"Life is complicated, my dear. I have the benefit of looking back over decades of life. Sometimes we have to face things we don't understand, and sometimes we have to forgive when it hurts, but we never truly know someone's heart until we talk to them, until we hear them tell their side of the story."

"But what if his truth hurts more?"

"Then you'll face it and you'll grow from it. But you'll never know if you don't talk to him. Don't let fear and anger rob you of your chance at happiness."

Heather nodded. Geneva's counsel had given her something to think about. It had helped her rise slightly above the anger that had been consuming her all day.

"Thank you," she whispered.

"You're always welcome here, Heather. Now, how about some pie to sweeten this bitter day?" Heather managed a weak smile. "I think I would like that."

Geneva moved around the kitchen slicing pie and pouring coffee. As Heather sat there with her mind filled with a storm of thoughts, she knew

Geneva was right. She needed to talk to Ethan to hear what his reasoning was.

Just as Geneva was about to place a nice piece of peach pie in front of her, there was a knock at the door. For a moment she worried that it was Ethan, that he had somehow figured out what she'd seen and he had followed her to Geneva's house, but instead it was Madeline.

"Oh, hey there, Madeline, come on in" Geneva said. Heather was surprised to see her. They had only met briefly at the inn before the search happened for the Lancaster family.

"You remember Heather?"

"Oh, of course," Madeline said, surprised to see somebody else sitting in the cabin. She looked like she wanted to turn around and leave, but she walked inside instead. "Nice to see you again, Heather." Madeline looked shaken up. She wondered if she'd had just the same kind of day that Heather had experienced.

"Goodness, you look terrible, too."

"Thanks a lot, Geneva," Madeline said with a laugh.

"Heather came because she's having a little challenging time in her life. It looks like you're having one in yours."

"A little bit, but I can talk to you about it later. I don't want to interrupt."

"Oh, don't be silly, we're just having a piece of pie and some coffee. I can cut another slice and pour another cup," Geneva said, smiling as she turned back to the kitchen.

Madeline took the bar stool next to Heather. They looked like two people drowning their sorrows in coffee. "So you had a rough day?" Madeline said.

"Yes, I found out that somebody close to me has been lying about something."

Madeline laughed under her breath. "It seems we're having the same issue."

"Oh dear. There's not something going on with you and Brady is there?" Geneva asked, sliding a cup of coffee and a piece of pie in front of Madeline.

"No, not Brady, but it's him I'm worried about."

"What happened?" Geneva asked. Madeline glanced over at Heather.

"Can we keep this between the three of us?"

Heather nodded quickly. "Of course, I'm not telling anybody anything."

"Well, as you know, Geneva, Jasmine is working as my assistant. She's doing a great job. I'm really happy to see her getting back on her feet. But when I went to make us lunch earlier, I walked back to ask her what kind of cheese she wanted on her sandwich, and I overheard her talking to her ex-husband on the phone."

"You mean the one who abused her and is in jail right now?" Geneva asked.

"That very one."

"Did you tell Brady?"

"Of course not. I don't want Brady to get himself into trouble. He would go straight down to that jail, and there's no telling what he would do, even if there are guards around."

"You're probably right about that. Did you confront her?"

"I did. She told me she's just having trouble with the cycle of abuse. She always went back to him, and she feels bad that he's begging her on the phone to come visit him or help him get out."

"Oh, no."

"I told her she's got to see her therapist to talk about this, and that she has to promise me that she'll change her phone number and she won't talk to him again."

"Do you think she'll do it?" Heather asked.

"I don't know. I can't say that I understand because I've never been through something like that, but I hope she listened to me. The thing is, she asked me not to tell Brady, and now I feel really guilty that I agreed to that."

"Well, it's probably best that he doesn't know," Geneva said.

"Really? I'm surprised at you, Geneva. I thought you would tell me to tell Brady."

"In a normal circumstance, I would, but Brady is a strong Southern man, and he is not going to abide an abuser, especially if he thinks that man is still talking to his sister."

"You're right. There's no telling what he will do."

"I think it's best that we just manage Jasmine on our own and don't let Brady know what's happened."

"Well, I'm glad to hear you say that. At least I feel like I'm not alone in this."

Geneva leaned across the counter and took each of their hands. "You girls are never alone in anything. As long as I'm the elder wise woman here in Jubilee, I feel it's my duty to make sure that I help you through the trials of your life," Geneva said, laughing.

"And we're glad you're here," Heather said.

If there was one place that Heather could go when she had heavy thoughts on her mind, it was Jubilee's local park. She loved to walk along the riverbank, looking at the ducks and hearing the sound of the leaves moving in the trees. She especially loved it during the fall, so she couldn't wait for the future weeks and months where she got to look at the orange leaves blowing.

But for now, it was still pretty hot outside. Thankfully, today, there was a bit of a breeze as she walked alone, trying to figure out how she felt about all the things going on right now. Of course, she was worried about the confrontation she was going to have with Ethan, but she was more thinking about her career. She had made such a split-second decision telling Nathan that she quit. The reality was she could call him up right now and get her job back because she knew Nathan believed she was a necessity in his business, but she didn't want to do that.

She didn't want to work there anymore, and now she had all of these things she needed to do, like get out of her apartment lease and tell all of her friends in the city goodbye. In reality, there really weren't that many good friends that she actually had. She had a lot of acquaintances, a lot of work friends, but nobody she would call a real friend.

Still, she wondered what was to become of her career now that she was going to be helping her mother at the inn. Was she going to slide into the role easily and then just run it for the rest of her life like Lanelle did? And who would she pass it on to one day if she didn't have kids of her own? What if her kids didn't want it? These were all questions that were rolling through her mind.

Heather tended to be the type that thought way too many steps ahead. She didn't think about just what was going on in the moment. She thought about ten or fifteen years from now, and that was not something that was a good idea.

As she continued to walk, she thought about how she could start her own freelance business and get her own clients. She had a lot of knowledge to give. Certainly, she could do it on the side, virtually, without having to go into an office every day. As she wandered deeper into the park, lost in thought, she noticed a figure sitting on a weathered bench up ahead. The man she saw was an integral part of her childhood memories, a constant presence in the park, like a timeless guardian of nature.

She knew his name was Burt, and he was probably in his seventies by now. His face was always etched with wisdom and kindness. His long gray beard and wise eyes made him look almost like a magical wizard from a fairy tale. He was a local legend known for his unique ability to hold his hands up full of birdseed and have birds, squirrels, and chipmunks come eat from his hands. He would let the little kids do it sometimes, too, and he was there every day. She wondered if he'd been there every day for all these years. Her heart warmed as she approached him, smiling. "Burt?" she called, her voice soft.

He looked up, his eyes twinkling a bit as he recognized her. "Heather? Wow, you've grown up! Come sit with me," he said, patting the bench beside him. Nobody knew where Burt lived. He always drove over there in his old truck. She didn't know what the model was or the year, but she could see it over in the parking lot. It still looked much the same. Dark blue with spots of primer on it. It was pretty beat up, but it looked like it was still running. Nobody ever knew exactly where he lived, and he didn't talk about his personal life. He liked to sit and just talk about mundane things and then feed his beloved animals.

She took a seat, her eyes drawn to a chipmunk that had boldly climbed right into Burt's lap. "You're still here feeding them after all these years."

Burt laughed, his eyes full of warmth, "They're my friends. They keep me company, teach me patience, and remind me to enjoy the simple things in life."

"I wish I could find such simplicity, Burt. Life feels so complicated right now."

His eyes met hers, filled with understanding. "Tell me, what weighs on your heart today?" Heather poured out many of her concerns, her worries about coming back to work at the inn, her decision to stay in Jubilee, her desire to balance the passion she had for her career with the love she had for her town and her mother.

She even shared some thoughts about starting her own business. He listened, his eyes never leaving her face, even if birds landed on his head and ate seed that he had placed on top of his hat.

When she was done, he looked out at the park, his expression thoughtful. "You know," he began, his voice gentle. "Nature has a way of finding balance. These trees, these animals, they all co-exist with each other. They all serve a purpose and they all find their place." He turned and looked at her, "Your place is here in Jubilee where your heart belongs. You have a gift, a talent for numbers and finance. You can use that to serve your community, to make the inn thrive, to help other people."

"But how? How do I find the balance? How do I make it all work?"

His smile was sincere. "Trust yourself, dear. Follow your heart and don't be afraid to take a chance. Just like these little friends of mine. They trust, they adapt, they find their way. They don't have to know upfront what's going to happen. They just show up here every day and expect that I'm going to be sitting here to feed them. But I know if one day I'm not here, they will find their way. They'll adapt. You have the strength and wisdom to find your way, Heather. Just embrace the challenge, follow your passion, and let your love for your family and Jubilee guide you."

Heather felt a surge of hope, a clarity she hadn't felt before. His words had reached her and ignited a fire within. "Thank you, Burt," she said. "I needed to hear that."

He patted her hand, "You knew it all along. You just needed a little reminder."

"Don't you ever get tired of coming here every day to feed the animals?"

He shook his head. "This is my place. I'm blessed to have found my place long ago."

She hugged him tightly, and as she walked away, her steps a little lighter, she knew what she had to do. She glanced back one more time, seeing Burt now standing by the river, both arms outstretched as four birds landed on his arms and started to eat the bird seed. He seemed to shimmer in the sunlight like a mystical beacon of wisdom.

CHAPTER 13

There were certain sounds associated with the morning chores that Madeline was getting accustomed to. The sound of hooves against hard dirt, the movement of buckets banging into each other.

This morning, she was helping Brady and Anna as they went about their chores. The air was filled with the scent of hay and the rich, earthy musk of animals. Anna was all excited as she regaled Brady and Madeline with stories of her new school.

"You won't believe it! I made three new friends already. And guess what? One of them invited me to her birthday party." Anna's voice was energetic and jubilant as she helped Brady with the feeding trough.

Madeline ruffled Anna's hair affectionately. "That's wonderful. Tell us everything about it."

As they worked, Anna chatted away, talking about her new friends, her teachers, the games they played at school, what she had learned, all the little things that made her day exciting. Brady and Madeline both listened, each of them happy for her finding her place in her new school.

Jasmine, who had been busy with other tasks unrelated to Madeline's business, eventually joined them. "So, Miss Popular, when is that party? I want all the details." Anna laughed. The family's chatter filled the barn. After a while, Jasmine's brow furrowed, and she turned to Brady, "Hey, Brady, the Wi-Fi is acting up again. Do you mind helping me figure it out?"

He wiped his hands on a rag. "Sure thing. Hey, Anna, you want to come inside and see if you can help me with a technical problem?"

“Okay,” she said, scampering away with him. It was only a half joke. It seemed like kids knew way more about technology than adults did these days.

As they continued the chores, Madeline's mind drifted to the troubling incident she had with Jasmine when she heard her on the phone with her ex-husband. It had been a few days now, and she wondered if Jasmine had kept her promise. There was just a concern and an unease that still stirred within her.

"Hey, Jasmine," she said, her voice soft as they spoke in the barn. "Have you talked to him anymore? Your ex, I mean."

Her eyes widened, "No. No, of course not. I swear, Madeline."

Madeline reached out and touched her arm, "I believe you. I just want to make sure you're okay. That's all."

Her eyes filled with tears, "Thank you. Thank you for understanding and for keeping it between us."

Unbeknownst to them, Brady had returned to the barn because he forgot his phone. Anna was trailing behind him, but she was completely oblivious to what was going on.

"Madeline," Brady's voice was sharp, filled with anger and betrayal. Madeline and Jasmine turned, both of their faces pale. Madeline's heart sinking. "You knew?" Brady's voice was low. His anger barely contained. "You knew she had talked to her ex, and you didn't tell me?"

"Brady, I didn't think it was my place, and

Jasmine asked me not to say anything. I wanted to respect her wishes."

His face twisted in pain, and his eyes were dark with hurt. "She's my sister. I had a right to know."

Jasmine stepped forward, "Brady, please understand. I was scared. I didn't want to worry you, and I didn't want you to do something rash."

"How could you keep this from me, Jasmine? Why would you even want to talk to that man?"

"That's my dad," Anna yelled out suddenly. Apparently, Brady had totally forgotten she was there.

He turned around and kneeled down, "Anna, this is an adult conversation. Why don't you go in the house and watch TV for a bit?" Her little shoulders fell as she turned around and went back toward the house. Brady then turned back toward Madeline and Jasmine. "You know, I can understand why Jasmine wouldn't tell me, but what about you, Madeline? We're supposed to be in love. I thought you would be honest with me about everything."

She walked forward, trying to touch his arm, but he backed up. "I just didn't want to break Jasmine's trust, and she promised me that she wouldn't talk to him anymore, that she would change her number."

"Do you really believe that? Do you really believe what she told you?"

"Excuse me," Jasmine said. "Quit talking about me like I'm not here. I made a promise, and I intend to keep it. In fact, I'm going to the cell phone store today to get my number changed."

Brady ran his fingers through his hair, aggravation on his face. "I need to go take a walk." As he walked away, Madeline felt completely helpless. She wanted to chase after him, explain again what had happened, but, instead, she just kept her feet planted in the barn. If he wanted some time alone, she wanted him to have it.

"I'm so sorry, Madeline," Jasmine said. "This is all my fault." Madeline knew that if Jasmine felt the weight of that guilt, she was likely to make a poor decision.

"No, it's not your fault. I shouldn't have agreed to keep it a secret. But you must keep your promise. You cannot talk to him anymore. If you do, I'm not sure what Brady might do."

"I understand, and I will keep my promise. Listen, I need to go check on my daughter."

As she watched Jasmine walk away, Madeline had never felt more alone in her life. She leaned against one of the stalls, only to have Gilbert stick his head through and nibble at her hip. It made her laugh for just a second, before tears started rolling down her cheeks.

HEATHER WALKED in the door of the inn fully expecting to see Ethan. She knew she needed to have this conversation with him, and it should be sooner rather than later. But again, he wasn't there. She walked into the living room to find her mother in the recliner, watching a TV show and doing a crossword puzzle. She was happy to see that her mom was finally relaxing. They were supposed to be getting new guests in another day or so, and her mother would be up on her feet running around as usual. She had no doubt about that.

"Hey, Mama," Heather said, flopping down on the sofa with a sigh.

"Oh, dear. You don't seem like you're in a very good mood."

"I just have a lot going on. Listen, I wanted to talk to you about something."

"Okay," Lanelle said, putting down her crossword puzzle and turning off the TV.

"I've made a decision about my career and Jubilee."

"You have?"

"Yes. I quit my job yesterday."

Lanelle's mouth dropped open. "You quit your job?"

"Yes. My boss was just being way too demanding, and he wanted me to come home when I wasn't ready."

"Oh, Heather, I'm so sorry I put you in that predicament. I didn't mean to."

"It's okay, Mama. I needed to do it. That man doesn't care anything about family, and I do."

"So what are you going to do now?"

"I'm going to work here with you," Heather said, forcing a smile and reaching over to touch her mother's hand.

"You are? But how is that going to fulfill you? You love your job."

"Well, I'm thinking about having a freelance business, something of my own, something where nobody else gets to tell me what to do."

Lanelle smiled. "I think that's a trait in our family, especially for the women. We don't like to be told what to do."

"It's going to be an adjustment for sure. But now

you don't have to worry about running this place alone. I'll be here. I need you to take care of your health. Drink more water. Take more time to rest."

"I feel like an old lady," Lanelle said, leaning her head back and closing her eyes. "It's a hard adjustment. It's almost like one day you just can't do some things anymore. But you keep trying, and then you end up hurting yourself."

"Well, you have to stop doing that. If we want this place to succeed, I'm going to need you at your best, and the way to get there is by taking care of yourself."

"I know. You're right."

"Well, I think I'm going to go make myself a little lunch and then take a walk."

"It seems like you've been walking all morning. What's going on?"

Heather stood up and walked toward the kitchen, turning around. "I just have a hard conversation I need to have with somebody."

"Anybody I know?"

Heather smiled slightly. "Mama, don't pry."

HEATHER SAT on the edge of Ethan's bed. He hadn't been home all day, and she didn't know where he was. The more she thought about it, the more she felt duped. She'd had men cheat on her in the past, but this felt even more egregious. It felt even more personal because it involved her mother. What Ethan was doing was going to affect her mother's business unless Heather could stop it. She felt like she didn't even know who he was.

Suddenly, she heard footsteps walking down the hallway. They were heavy, and she knew they had to be Ethan's. The door opened, and he saw her sitting there on his bed, holding his file folder in her lap. She stared at him, and he stopped in the doorway, slowly closing the door behind him.

"Heather, what are you doing in here?"

"The better question is what is this, Ethan?" Her voice was trembling with rage as she held up the file. His eyes widened.

"Heather, I can explain."

"Explain? You've been spying on me, on my family, on this inn, maybe even on this town. I thought you cared about me, about Jubilee. Was all of that a lie?"

His face fell. His eyes filled with pain and guilt. "No, Heather, it wasn't a lie. I do care about you a lot, and I love Jubilee, and I care about your mom. But I was here for another reason too."

"A reason? What could possibly be a good reason to justify betraying us?"

He looked down. "I am a writer and a historian. That part is true, but I was hurting for money, and I was hired by someone, an investor who was interested in buying the inn. He saw that your mother was struggling to keep up the payments on her loans. He wanted me to investigate the place, investigate the town, find out if this was a viable purchase."

Heather's heart felt like it stopped, like the words were punching her in the gut. "You were investigating us for a buyer? What did he want to do with the place?"

"He was hoping to eventually buy up most of the shops on this street, tear them down, and build a strip mall."

Heather's mouth dropped open. "Oh, my gosh. That would be the worst thing in the world for Jubilee."

"Yeah, and because the inn takes up such a large space, even if he couldn't buy anything else, he was able to come up with a plan for tearing this down and building a two-story office building here."

"Tearing down the inn, and you were going to help him do this?"

"I wasn't helping him do that. I was just investigating, just finding out if it was a viable option."

"So where have you been every day? You weren't really at the courthouse."

"I was at the courthouse. Sometimes I was actually studying up on the town. I do want to write a book about small towns but a lot of times, I was looking at the records, poring over plat maps, that sort of thing."

"I can't believe this. I really trusted you." She stood up and walked across the room, her arms crossed.

"Heather, I never expected to fall for you and to fall for this town. I never expected to feel the way I do. And once I felt that way, I wasn't going to go through with it. I was going to tell you today. I swear."

She laughed. "Really? You were going to tell me? When were you going to tell me? After you sold us out to the investor, after you'd given him whatever information he needed to ruin my family's legacy?"

He reached his hand out, trying to touch her, but she pulled back. "Heather, please, let me explain more. Let me make this right."

"Make it right? How could you possibly make this right, Ethan? You betrayed me. You betrayed my family. You betrayed this town. You put all of us at risk."

Ethan's voice broke. "I know, Heather. I know. But I'll do whatever it takes to make this right. I'll help you figure out how to pay off the loans. I'll do whatever I can to save the inn."

She looked at him, almost growling with her words. "I don't need your help. I don't need anything from you."

Her heart ached as she looked at him. She still cared about him. She had wanted to believe him, to trust him, but this wound felt too deep right now. "I can help you. I can fix this."

"You can't fix this. You can't undo what you've done."

She walked toward the door. "Please let me try. Let me prove to you that I'm not the person you think I am right now."

She turned and looked at him. "It's too late. You have shown me who you are, and I would never trust you again." As she walked down the hallway, she wondered if she had just given up on a great possible relationship, but how could she ever trust a man who would do something like that and not tell her?

ANNA RAN UP AHEAD of Brady, Madeline, and Jasmine.

"Here it is!" she exclaimed, pointing to a painting of a bright sunflower. "I made it for all of you."

Jasmine's eyes filled with tears as she looked at her daughter's artwork. "It's beautiful, Anna, just like you."

Anna had only been in school for a little over a week now, but the school had decided to have an art show, showcasing all the artwork the kids had done in the first week. They wanted the parents to be excited to see their progress at the end of the year when they had their second art show.

"You did an incredible job, sweetie. I'm so proud of you," Brady said.

Madeline's eyes met Brady's, but his gaze was still distant, his body language still stiff. They had hardly spoken since the incident at the barn. She felt a pang of sadness. She was happy about Anna's success at school, but she hated this lingering tension between her and Brady.

As the family mingled with other parents and children enjoying the community and celebration, a minor mishap occurred. Anna accidentally knocked over a glass of red punch, staining another child's artwork. Her face turned bright red, tears welling in her eyes.

"It's okay, honey," Brady reassured her. "Accidents happen. We'll help clean it up."

Together, they worked as a family to fix the situation, including supporting Anna through her embarrassment. She was new at the school, and this was one of the worst things that could happen to an eight-year-old little girl.

When the event drew to a close, Madeline felt a growing sense of urgency. She needed to address this tension with Brady. She pulled him aside in the parking lot while Jasmine and Anna were talking to another family.

"Brady, we need to talk. I can't go on like this, with you avoiding me and giving me the cold shoulder."

His jaw tightened. "You kept something very important from me, Madeline. How can I trust you not to do that again?"

"I know, and I'm sorry. I didn't mean to betray your trust. I was trying to protect your sister, and I was trying to protect you."

"You were trying to protect me? How? By keeping a secret? By lying?"

"It wasn't a lie, Brady. It was a mistake. Can't you see that? Can't you forgive me? I really was trying to keep you from going over to that jail and doing something stupid."

"Do you really think I'm that big of an idiot? I'm a grown man, Madeline. You don't think I can control my emotions?"

"I didn't know what you would do. I know you love your sister, and I knew if you thought she was talking to him again, it would ruin the relationship you're trying to build with her. So I made a deal with her that she wouldn't talk to him anymore, that she would change her phone number, which she has done, and she would put a restraining order against him so he didn't come around if and when he gets out of jail."

Brady sighed. "I understand why you did it. I just need to know from now on that I can trust you, that you'll be honest with me, no matter what, that you will trust me to know how to handle my own emotions."

She looked down and then back at his face, walking over and taking both of his hands. "I promise, Brady. I'll never keep anything from you again, unless it's what I got you for Christmas or your birthday. I value our relationship too much to risk it. But, please, can we move past this?"

Brady's eyes finally softened, his body language relaxing. "Yes, we can move past it. I want this tension to be gone."

He pulled her into a tight embrace, and Madeline had never felt so relieved in her life.

CHAPTER 14

Heather watched out the window as Ethan's car pulled away from the inn, disappearing down the winding road. She felt a pang of sadness. His departure had been abrupt and tense, to say the least. She couldn't believe this was the way things had ended.

The romantic part of her thought that when she decided to stay in Jubilee that maybe he would do the same or at least offer to come visit for extended periods. Instead, she found out about his deceit and she just couldn't trust him. Her mother and the inn were now the most important things in her life as they always should have been, and she just could not have Ethan interfering in that.

She dusted herself off and pushed aside all the

conflicting emotions. There was work to be done, lots of work. The inn was in dire straits financially, and it was up to her to pull it back from the brink. After all, she was experienced in the finance industry. Surely she would be able to figure this out and save the family's legacy. She had a newfound sense of determination, but it was probably caused by the fact that she was trying to distract herself from watching Ethan leave.

She made her way to the office, her mind racing with ideas. The loans were substantial, but they weren't insurmountable. She would just have to be creative and relentless. She began by poring over the financial records, looking for areas where expenses could be cut without sacrificing quality, ordering in bulk, renegotiating with some of their suppliers, eliminating unnecessary luxuries. She was meticulous and thorough. She left no stone unturned. Next, she looked into the marketing strategies. She realized that the inn's online presence was pretty inadequate. She revamped the website, adding more professional and eye-catching images, and then she created some new content to hopefully draw in potential guests.

Social media accounts were updated, and then she placed them on the calendar so that she wouldn't forget to post more often. She looked into doing paid advertising, but that would have to wait for now. And then she started a blog about the inn's unique charm and their family history. She put information about all the different shops and linked to the websites of Perky's, The Rustic Spoon and The Buzzed Bear. Of course, she also linked to the bookstore's website since it was one of her favorite places in town. After many hours in the office, she needed a break. She made herself a list of some other things she needed to do, like reaching out to wedding planners.

She started to sketch out some tailored packages where she would collaborate with local vendors to provide everything from photography to catering.

"Honey, you're working yourself to death." Lanelle said after Heather didn't come out for lunch.

"There's a lot to do, Mama."

"I know that, but why don't you come eat a bite? Your blood sugar's going to get too low, and you're going to feel terrible." Heather laughed. Her mother had always threatened low blood sugar, but Heather didn't know if she had ever felt that in her entire life.

"I'll be there in a minute."

"Hurry up. I made soup, and you don't want it to get cold."

Heather could smell her mother's vegetable soup from the kitchen. It was one of her favorite things she made. Heather remembered when she was a little kid and would come home from school not feeling well with a cold. Her mother would make vegetable soup and put extra garlic in it. She said it would cure her.

Heather closed the laptop and laid her head on it. There was so much going on, so many possibilities, but her heart ached. She didn't know why she felt so strongly for Ethan after such a short time. Maybe she was just being overly dramatic. Maybe she was just wishing for that life she'd never got to lead. The one with the picket fence and the little children running underfoot. Maybe she was getting too old for that.

Now, in her mid thirties, it seemed awfully late to be starting a family. All of her friends already had kids, at least in middle school and some in high school. Heather felt left behind, but she wasn't going to push it by getting into a relationship with someone unless she was truly in love. She wasn't going to bring children into the world unless she had a solid marriage. And right now, that seemed like something that was so far away and completely out of reach for her.

MADELINE DIDN'T KNOW why she was so nervous about this book signing. It was at Away With Words, which was obviously a comfortable place for her, but she hadn't done a book signing in well over a year. She used to do them all around the world with hordes of readers coming to meet her. Clemmy had invited her to do a signing with some of her older books so they could give some of the proceeds to Lanelle. They wanted to help her pay off the loan for All Tucked Inn. Everybody in town wanted to make sure the inn was preserved, and that it was able to stay in the Callaway family for generations to come.

The rich aroma of coffee mingled with the scent of the freshly printed books as Madeline walked over to the table and sat down. Jasmine was there to help as well, and Madeline was glad for it. Having an assistant again, especially somebody that she didn't have to worry about cheating on her or cheating with her husband, had been a godsend. She was busy organizing stacks of books and brochures about the inn. She'd put the word out on social media, so readers were coming from miles around.

"Madeline, you look radiant," Clemmy exclaimed as she walked over and hugged her. "I'm so glad we're doing this. This is a wonderful cause to support."

Madeline smiled. "I couldn't think of a better place and, yes, Lanelle needs all the help she can get. I don't know her as well as I plan to, but she seems like a wonderful woman."

Jasmine walked up, her face glowing with enthusiasm. "The turnout really looks promising. Lots of people on social media are buzzing about it, and they love that you're helping the inn." A few moments later, the doors opened, and the crowd began to filter in.

Clemmy and Jasmine tag-teamed to make sure that everybody got their moment with Madeline. Lots of people wanted autographs, of course, but many wanted to also have their pictures taken.

Madeline felt her heart swelling with gratitude when she saw the familiar faces of people from Jubilee, but also lots of new ones. Many of these readers had read her books for years. Somehow along the way, she had forgotten just how popular her books used to be. She had lost her confidence, but she was quickly gaining it back when she saw the crowd. As the signing got underway, Madeline found herself immersed in engaging conversations with readers.

Some of them shared stories about how her books had touched their lives over the years. Others told her that they read her books while they were taking chemotherapy and how it had helped them get through. Many of them wanted to know more about how they could help the inn and if they could even donate extra money directly. Jasmine and Clemmy handled all the sales quickly so that each person got their time with Madeline. Clemmy also mingled with the crowd, sharing information about the inn and encouraging more people to visit Jubilee. One reader in particular had talked to Madeline about starting her own writing career. She told Madeline that her books had inspired her to pursue her writing dreams.

Madeline had forgotten just how important it was for her to interact with her readers. It made her feel so much better about the future of her career. As the afternoon wore on and the crowd continued to grow, the energy in the room was palpable. It was electric. Brady stopped by to see her, but she was far too busy signing books and taking pictures to spend much time with him. Anna also came, adding to the festive atmosphere. She explored the bookstore and picked out several books to purchase before heading home.

Brady walked over to Madeline and whispered in her ear, "You're doing something incredible here. Lanelle is lucky to have you."

She looked up at him. "Well, we're all family in Jubilee, right? We take care of each other."

The event wasn't without its challenges. There was a mix-up with a delivery that threatened to disrupt the flow, but Jasmine had handled everything with grace and efficiency, ensuring that everything ran as smoothly as possible. As the day ended, and the final count was tallied, the amount raised was beyond everyone's expectations. In fact, when Clemmy announced the total, the room erupted in cheers. Even Heather stopped by, and when she heard how much was being given to the inn, she started crying. It was going to pay off at least one of the final loans they were dealing with. Madeline stood up in front of the last group of readers and decided to say something. She felt like she needed to thank her readers for coming out to support the inn.

"Thank you all for being here today and for supporting not just my work but a piece of Jubilee's heart. All Tucked Inn is more than an inn. It's a family legacy that you're helping to preserve. Your generosity means more than you know. So from the bottom of my heart, thank you."

Everyone applauded and Madeline felt tears welling in her eyes. Not only had the community come together, but the reader community had also done the same. As the guests began to disperse, Madeline, Clemmy, and Jasmine gathered for a moment.

"We did it," Jasmine said, her eyes shining brightly.

"We really made a difference." Clemmy hugged both women tightly. "This is what Jubilee is all about, friendship, community, and love. We take care of our own."

They spent the next hour cleaning up, sharing laughter, each one knowing they had been a part of something very special. As Madeline drove back to her cabin, she let out a contented sigh, a smile on her face and a song in her heart, as the Jubilee town square disappeared in her rear-view mirror, and she headed toward her mountain home.

HEATHER'S HANDS were shaking as she clutched the pink piece of paper. The numbers on the page were clear, cold and merciless. They had one week. That's all the time they had to pay off the remaining loan on the inn. She just couldn't figure out how things had come to this. Normally, Lanelle would've used a local bank in Jubilee, but she had exhausted all of her options when she took out this loan. It was a national bank, and they didn't care that this was a family legacy about to go up in smoke.

The loan was the largest of the ones she had taken out, and it seemed impossible that they would find a way to pay it off in a week. Heather planned to go to the local bank tomorrow to see if there was any way she could get a new loan to pay off the other one. It felt like robbing Peter to pay Paul, like she was rearranging deck chairs on the Titanic. She didn't want her mother to know that this notice had come in the mail, but she was going to have to tell her they had one week to finish paying it off. The inn was collateral, which meant that they could take it anytime after that.

She paced around the room, her mind a whirlwind of thoughts, fears and desperation. Lanelle was getting better, drinking more water and taking time for herself. The inn was even starting to do well. They had more guests coming than ever and she was setting up all kinds of future promotions and events, but maybe it was all going to be too late. That last loan was a dark cloud looming over their heads, threatening to rain down chaos on everything they had built and were building.

"That piece of paper is from the bank, isn't it?" Lanelle said from behind her.

"You weren't supposed to see this," Heather responded, putting it on the desk and covering it up with something, like that was going to make a difference.

"We'll figure something out, darling," Lanelle reassured her. "We always do. This inn has had many challenges over its lifetime."

"Let's be real. This inn has never been this close to being lost out of our family, and Lord knows what they'll do with the land and the building if we lose it. I knew we should have pursued getting this registered with the historic register a long time ago."

"Well, we still have time."

"No, Mama, we don't. That paper says we have one week, and that's the biggest loan. How in the world are we going to pay that off in a week?"

"I don't know, but I do know that God has a way of working things out."

"Well, I wish I had your faith in that. I've done everything I can think to do, and it just hasn't been good enough. It seems I came home too late." Lanelle walked over and hugged her daughter. There wasn't much she could say that was going to make Heather feel better. Right now she felt like the entire world was caving in. "You know, I'm going to give them a call. Maybe they will extend it if I give them our sob story," Heather said.

"Maybe so. I'm going to go make a pot of coffee because I think this might be a long day," Lanelle said, kissing her daughter on the cheek and walking out of the room. Heather was pretty sure her mom didn't want to hear this. It had to be stressful for her. Heather dialed the number on the pink slip of paper. It had arrived in the mail a few days ago, but she had just gotten the courage to open it up.

The woman answered, and Heather began to speak. "Hi, this is Heather Callaway. We own All Tucked Inn and we have a loan with you. We got a pink slip of paper that says we have one week to take care of this from the date that we received the paper, and by my calculation..."

Before she could finish her sentence, the woman interrupted her. "Is this the inn that is located in Jubilee, Georgia?"

"Yes, it is."

"Well, I have good news for you. Just this morning, that loan was paid off in full."

"What?" Heather stammered, her mind reeling. "How? Who?"

The woman paused for a moment. "I'm not at liberty to say, but everything is settled. You have nothing to worry about. You'll be getting a notice in the mail showing that it's completely paid off."

Heather ended the call without saying anything else, her heart pounding. She was relieved, of course, but she was very confused. Who would've done this, and why?

As the weeks passed, Heather eased into life in Jubilee again. Today she was taking a walk on the square. Everything at the inn had changed seemingly overnight when that loan was paid off. Her mother appeared to be so much more energetic and happy. They had new guests coming almost every day and they could barely keep up, such that they had to create a waiting list. There was already a wedding planned for the next spring, and Heather was working with several other wedding planners. Things had really turned around quickly, but none of it could have happened without that loan being paid off. She wondered who it was, but the benefactor had not made themselves known at this point. She would just have to live in the mystery, she supposed.

Her freelance business was also picking up. George Jennings, her biggest client, had decided to continue working with her instead of Nathan. As soon as his contract was up next month, he would be a client of Heather's new firm. That alone would give her plenty of work to do and lots of extra income to keep her stable.

She got a coffee at Perky's and then walked over to the bookstore where Clemmy was behind the counter. She had a big smile on her face when Heather walked in.

"I think I know why you're here," she said grinning.

Heather stared at her confused. "You do?

"Well, I assume so," Clemmy said, looking confused herself.

"I don't know what you're talking about. I was just taking a little break after lunch and thought I'd get a coffee. You know I like to come poke around the bookstore whenever I get a chance."

Clemmy's mouth dropped open slightly. "Wait. You mean you really don't know?" Clemmy quickly sent a text on her phone, which seemed odd to Heather.

"Really don't know what? Have you been taking some new medication or something?"

Clemmy laughed. "No. I guess I just thought you'd heard by now."

"Clemmy, can you please tell me what you're talking about? This is exhausting."

"Instead of me telling you, why don't I show you?" Clemmy said, walking out from behind the counter. She walked over to a table and picked up a book, handing it to Heather. On the front was a picture of the courthouse. It was a book about the town of Jubilee.

"Wait, what is this? Somebody wrote a book about Jubilee?"

"Yeah. Somebody you know," Clemmy said.

Heather looked back down and there it was, Ethan's name. "I don't want this," Heather said handing it back to her.

"Now listen, I know what happened, but I think you need to read some of that, or at least the first page."

"Why would I read the first page? This guy came to our town and was deceitful to all of us."

"I think there's more to the story, though."

"Well, I don't think so. I haven't even heard from him since he left."

"What did you expect him to say?"

"I don't know. I suppose I thought he would apologize."

"I think he already apologized, didn't he? That's what you told me."

"Well, he did, but there are never too many apologies."

Clemmy chuckled. "Heather, for once in your life, don't argue with me. Just open it up and look at the first page."

Heather sighed and put her coffee down before opening the book. The first page was a dedication, and it read, "*To the people in the town of Jubilee, Georgia, thank you for welcoming me. Thank you for being the type of community that makes others want to move there. Jubilee is a special place and it just can't be duplicated anywhere else because of the people and the places and the beautiful, majestic mountains. Jubilee is now my favorite place on earth as it is also home to one of my favorite people. Heather, I'm sorry for what happened and I hope that when I come back to Jubilee next time, you'll sit down and have a cup of coffee with me.*"

Heather just stared at the book. She didn't understand what she was reading. "Okay, so he wrote a dedication in a book. That's not really going to fix the problem, is it?" she said, handing the book back to Clemmy and picking up her coffee.

"That's not all."

"What do you mean?"

Clemmy looked at her. "I get the feeling that you don't know the full story about what this book means."

"And you would be right about that. I don't know what this book means other than he wrote a nice book about Jubilee and he's going to make some good money off of it, I guess."

Clemmy rolled her eyes. "You know, you need to be more forgiving."

"Excuse me?"

"You want other people to forgive you for things? Then you need to forgive them for things."

"Clemmy, where is all of this coming from?"

Clemmy threw her hands up in the air. "Okay, I'm going to spell it out for you. Ethan called last week and asked if we would carry these books at the bookstore. He told me a secret, and he told me not to tell you, but here I go. He got this book deal from his publisher specifically because he told them he needed an advance, and he would write this book. They gave him enough of an advance so that he could call and pay off that loan. He worked night and day to get this book finished, and his publisher sped up the publication."

Suddenly, Heather felt like somebody had kicked her in the stomach. "Wait. Ethan's the one who paid off the loan?"

"Yes, he did, and he didn't want credit for it. He wrote this book and wanted us to carry it here just so you could see that he wasn't as terrible of a person as you thought he was. He told the guy who hired him to do all the research on the town and the inn that he wasn't going to allow him to buy any property here. So the only thing he knew to do was to get an advance on the book and spend it on that loan. He's not going to make any money off this book."

Heather was stunned. She couldn't believe it. Nobody had ever done anything so nice like that before. Even though Ethan had not told her the full truth at first, in the end, he had actually been the one to save the place, to save her family legacy.

"Oh, my gosh. I can't believe anyone did a grand gesture like that for us. I don't know what to do."

"Well, you could start by turning around," Clemmy said.

When Heather turned around, she saw Ethan

standing there behind her holding a bouquet of red roses. "Ethan, what are you doing here?"

He smiled. "Well, I had planned to come over to the inn today and beg you to stop hating me, but you happened to show up here before I could do that. I had to hide in the storage room."

Clemmy smiled as she looked at the two of them, and then she slipped away out of sight to give them their time alone.

"I saw the book."

"Yeah, I heard the whole thing. Clemmy wasn't supposed to tell you about me paying off the loan."

"Thank you for what you did for me and my mom, for our family. It means more than you'll ever know."

"Listen, I would've done anything to get you to speak to me again and know that I'm not as bad a guy as you think I am."

She smiled slightly. "I might've been overly stressed at the time. I don't think you're a bad guy, Ethan."

"That's a relief to hear," he said, stepping forward. "These are for you."

She took the flowers and smelled one of the roses. She had always loved them. They were her favorite flower. "Thank you. So what does this mean?"

He shrugged his shoulders. "I guess it means whatever you want it to mean. All I can tell you is that I believe in the inn, I believe in you, and I believe in Jubilee so much that I've rented a place here."

Her eyes opened wide. "You've rented a place?"

"Yes, and not because of you totally. Of course, my plan was to try to woo you back by just being around all the time."

She laughed. "I'm not sure that would've worked as well as this."

"Well, just know that I'm in Jubilee, and I would like to see what we can build together, if you're interested."

She grinned. "I'm very interested, and I'm going to pay you that money back."

He held up his hand and shook his head. "Absolutely not. There will be no paying back that money. Agreed?"

"I feel terrible that you lost your advance."

"Well, don't feel bad because I gained so much more in the process."

He stepped forward and pressed his lips to hers. As Heather put her arms around his neck, she couldn't believe that this was how her story was going. Just like one of Madeline's romance books. She never thought that was possible, but now she had decided to be open to all the possibilities because sometimes dreams really did come true.

EPILOGUE

Madeline loved the fall. It was her favorite time of the year no matter where she was, but she definitely loved it in the Blue Ridge Mountains. Today she had a day off from writing, and she had enjoyed herself immensely. She was one of those people who didn't mind spending time alone, and today was just one of those days where the temperature outside was perfect and the view was even better.

As she stood in her living room, a cup of coffee keeping her hands warm, she looked out the giant windows over the mountain view. Looking at the trees in all of their orange splendor was one of her favorite things to do. She loved to watch the leaves fall and see the bright blue sky behind the orange glow of the treetops. Even the air outside was crisp and had a hint of smokiness to it. Yes, fall was her favorite time of the year.

Today, Brady had taken Anna on a trail ride. Jasmine had gone along too, wanting to make sure that her brother didn't let her little girl fall off the horse anywhere along the way. Madeline could have gone, but she told them to go without her. She was learning to ride a horse, and she enjoyed it most of the time, but today she just wanted to spend some time alone getting things done. She did a little organizing in her office, messed around with a few recipes after lunch, and now she was just enjoying the view.

So much about her life had changed since she moved to Jubilee. It seemed like every week she added new friends that became family. Geneva was the one closest to her, probably followed by Clemmy. She respected the two older women and loved to listen to their advice and stories. Clemmy was out on a nature hike with some kids from the local school. She had gone on several hikes with Geneva, and she had enjoyed them all.

Madeline had also enjoyed becoming a surrogate grandmother to Anna. She got to see her most days and heard about all the fun things she was doing at school. Even though she had never had any kids of her own, Anna was filling a void she didn't even know she had. And since Anna didn't have any grandparents, Madeline took that job seriously. She loved to bake cookies with her and take her shopping. They watched silly movies together, and sometimes they rode on the golf cart down to get the mail.

The feeling of family was something that Madeline had longed for most of her life. She had a fairly decent family herself until she got older and became a romance author. Her mother had not approved of her profession at all. She thought it was a silly way to make a living. She hadn't spoken to her mother in so many years, and she felt bad about it at times, but she knew that she hadn't done anything wrong. She was just living her life, and it became too hard to have a relationship with her mother if she was going to be so critical about her choice of profession. Madeline was proud of what she did. She got emails and fan mail all the time with people telling her how her books changed their lives. She could never be embarrassed of that.

She walked over and sat down in her favorite armchair, thinking about the upcoming holiday season. She couldn't wait to have Thanksgiving and

Christmas in Jubilee. What a fun time that was going to be to see all the decorations in town, go to the Christmas parade, and even to the tree lighting. She couldn't wait to decorate the cabin and see what it looked like during the holiday season. Everything was going to be brand new to her, and she was excited about that.

Just as she was dozing off in her chair, she heard a knock at the door. She put the coffee cup on her end table and stood up, walking over to the door as she pulled her cardigan tighter around her. It was time to turn up the heat as it was getting cooler in the mountains. When she opened the door, she couldn't believe what she saw. Her mother was standing there looking at her.

"Mom? What are you doing here?" she asked, her eyes wide.

"I came here to save you from yourself," she said, pushing past Madeline and walking into the house.

Maybe the holiday season wasn't going to be as joyous after all.

CHECK out all of my books at store. rachelhannaauthor.com.

Made in the USA
Middletown, DE
22 September 2023